#BOOMERISDONNAS

BOOMER

RUTHLESS KINGS MC
BOOK TWO

K.L. SAVAGE

ISBN: 978-1-952500-02-2
LIBRARY OF CONGRESS CONTROL: 2020906815

PHOTOGRAPHY BY WANDER AGUIAR PHOTOGRAPHY
COVER MODEL: KAZ VAN DER WAARD
COVER DESIGN: LORI JACKSON DESIGN
EDITING: MASQUE OF THE RED PEN
FORMATTING: CHAMPAGNE BOOK DESIGN

SECOND EDITION PRINT 2020

To all my readers who feel unseen.
You're more than a beautiful ornament broken on the floor.
You may feel like everyone walks around you, not noticing you, and leaving you to your own demise. I've lived in darkness, and it's okay to ask for help. One day, those beautiful pieces will be put together again.

AUTHOR'S NOTE

To Jamie O, one of my badass readers,

I wanted to reach out to you and tell you how much I appreciated your review. It was beautiful, poetic, and the perfect analogy to describe Boomer. I always try to put a bit of myself in all the characters, and Boomer holds a special place in my heart because I gave him a part of me that no other character has gotten before.

All those broken bits that made Boomer who he was, make up parts of me too.

The first sentence of your review inspired me. I used this sentence to help write the dedication in Boomer's story. *"You ever see a beautiful ornament broken on the floor everyone walks around it but no one sees it? That's Boomer."*

Thank you for your kind words. I appreciate them dearly, and I know the men and women of the Ruthless Kings appreciate it too. Thank you for reading, and I hope you continue to read the series. I look forward to more of your reviews. Tool will need your attention soon ☺

Stay ruthless, Jamie,
K.L. Savage

PROLOGUE

Boomer

I'M LOST.

My mind is lost, my heart, my soul. I don't know where to start looking for it, and I have no idea when the journey will end. Growing up in the MC hasn't left me feeling like I belong. I feel the opposite. It started when my father, Hawk, died on a run when I was young. Ever since then, part of me has darkened, and I haven't been able to find myself.

I'm angry.

I'm depressed.

And I have no idea where I belong in life. What's sad is I don't feel like it's here with the people who have loved and raised me. I feel guilty about it, but I need to do this for me. I need to find myself. I need to know who I am without the MC. I haven't been good to anybody here. I'm lashing out. I'm rude.

I know I am.

I haven't forgiven Reaper for what happened to my dad. I should. It was so long ago. So much of my life changed. He died. I gained a sister I had no idea existed. I got shot, and then I got kidnapped, shot again, and I lost a fucking finger. The only good thing to come of that was Sarah.

I know what I'm about to do will leave her broken. She'll hate me, but I'm prepared for that. I'll have to learn to live with it like I've learned to live with everything else. I'm drowning here. I can barely breathe. Every day here feels like I'm being pushed under water, struggling and fighting to gain that quick second of breath.

I'm tired.

I need to find happiness within myself, or I'll never be a good person, a better brother, or a better son to Reaper. I don't know if I'll ever find what I'm looking for, but something has to fill this void inside me. If I don't, I'm afraid of what I'll be.

What I'll turn into.

If I give into the dark thoughts that swirl inside my mind over and over again, that could ruin the man I am. Part of me wonders if I'm better off dead, if I'm better off not existing in this world, but I know that's the void in me talking. It isn't who I am, and I want to beat it. I want to conquer it, and I can't do that here.

The only thing I have done is piss people off, and I'm tired of it. I'm better off on my own. Even if I've never been on my own, I've felt like I have been all these years. The MC is better off without me, and right now, I think I'm better off without them.

It doesn't mean I won't miss any of them.

Like Tongue's crazy obsession with his knives, or the way Bullseye is impossible to beat at darts. I'll miss Pirate's rum drinking and Tank's soft heart. It always makes me chuckle to know a big man like that is a teddy bear. I'll miss Tool and his ability to fix anything and everything. He's the only reason why I have my dad's bike.

I'll miss my sister and her crazy ways.

I'll miss Reaper too, even if most of me blames him. I'll still miss the man who raised me. Just because I love everyone and will miss them, it isn't reason enough for me to stay. People find themselves and who they trust once they enter the MC because it's the thing they have been looking for.

Trust, love, family. A brotherhood. Through blood and fucking death, the Ruthless Kings have one another's backs. It's remarkable, commendable, and honorable.

And while I have all that, something is missing. I'm fucked up. I have something great, I know, and here I am saying it isn't enough. It isn't because it isn't enough that I need to leave. It's me. I'm the one who isn't enough.

Not for the club.

Not for fucking anybody.

I take one last look around my room, the place I've called home for nearly my entire life, and let out a heavy sigh. Everything is still here. My bed, my comforter, the half-naked posters of models on the wall, and the one part of the wall where Sarah wrote in red sharpie, "I love you, cranky." My heart twists knowing I won't see her for a while. I pull out my phone and take a picture of it so I can look at it whenever I want.

I'll miss her the most. I never knew I wanted a sister until I found out she and I share the same father. I swore I'd protect her with my life, and I have. She doesn't need me anymore. She has Reaper. Another thing I'm trying to come to terms with; their love. It's hard to look at the two of them sometimes because she is young, and he's so fucking old. I mean, late thirties isn't that old but hell, when the woman you're spending your life with is eighteen, you're fucking old.

Maybe it's just me.

My bed creaks as I stand, my weight causing the springs to groan as it releases. I know I have everything. I've triple checked a hundred times. Everything I need, I have in the backpack that's slung over my shoulder. Clothes and a few pictures that I had on my dresser. One of me and Sarah, another of all of us on her prom night all dressed up to the nines, and then the last one is of me and Reaper.

My dad had just died, and it was hard on me. He took me fishing and, in the picture, he was soaking wet from jumping in and grabbing the fish, and he helped me hold the flopping trout. It was my favorite memory. I got a hook caught in me that trip, in the finger that asshole Fabian chopped off when he left me hanging in an underground warehouse.

I fucking loved fishing with Reaper.

Not that I have ever told him that; my pride—or my anger, whichever it is—always gets in the way.

Pushing the memories to the back of my mind is like forgetting how to take steps—it just doesn't happen, but I have to. I grab the keys off the dresser and step out the door, turning to look over my shoulder. I reach up, and my fingers roam over the light switch. This is it.

At the same time, I release a breath and turn off the light, encompassing my past in darkness. My father's boots echo lightly with every thud against the floorboards of the clubhouse as I walk toward church. I honestly didn't realize I'd get emotional doing this.

I've been ready to leave, and now that I am, it's hitting

harder than I thought it would. My eyes burn with tears that I know I'll cry at some point, but not today. I can't today, or I won't make it out that damn door.

It's around four in the morning, and the clubhouse is quiet since everyone is sleeping. I pass by Pirate, passed out drunk on the couch, and I roll my eyes when I see his hands down his pants and his shirt off. His chest has hickeys all over it from one of the cut-sluts.

Once I'm safely out of Pirate's way, I open the church doors and lay my bag gently on the floor by the door. *This room.* My fists clench. Fuck, this room. Every decision ever made by the club has been held in this room, including the one that got my father killed.

Stop being so angry.

I can't! I can't stop. It eats away at me. It's killing me slowly. I either want to die or someone needs to, by my hands. I feel like it's the only way for this to get better, for the darkness to fade away.

But I know no matter what, the shadows inside me will always be there.

Shrugging off my father's cut, I lay it on the long mahogany table with the Ruthless Kings symbol carved in the middle and the skeleton gavel laying directly in front of the President's chair. Rumor has it, it's carved out of the first enemy one of the Ruthless Kings killed. Who knows, maybe it's true; it sure looks like it. How Reaper grabs that knowing it's made of a human being is something I can barely stomach.

My eyes drift back to the cut on the table, worn and ragged; this thing has seen hell. Damn, my father lived and died in this thing. It's torn and old. The only thing new about it is the prospect patch on it. I rub my finger over it and remember a time when I couldn't wait to have this patch. It was a short time, but I remember it well.

The material scratches the pad of my finger, and it sounds like sandpaper against a slab of wood from all the callouses I have after long hours in the garage. I shut my eyes, swallow the lump in my throat, and take a seat in the leather chair. To my left is a notepad and pen, and I plan to use it.

I'm writing one letter, and that's to Sarah.

I clear my throat and reach for the pen with a shaky hand while sliding the paper in front of me. No need for me to alert everyone by flipping the light switch; I can work from the dull glow creeping in the window.

With a deep breath, I put the pen to paper and let my thoughts flow.

Hey kid,

I don't know how to say this. I've been running it over and over in my head, trying to find the right words, but there aren't any. By the time you read this, I'll be long gone. Don't think for one second this is because of you. It ain't. How I feel has nothing to do with you, Sarah. I just need time to clear my head. The MC has clouded it. It's all I've known for as long as I can remember, and I can't remember any of it being good. I left dad's cut for you. Wear it. You deserve it more than I do. The MC isn't something I'm proud of, not yet, and that's the journey I need to go on—to see if the club is more than I think it is.

I hope you understand. I don't know when I'll be back but live well.

I love you. I'll miss the fuck out of you.

Your brother,

Jenkins

BOOMER

Damn, that's short. Reading the words makes it seem like I haven't said enough. She deserves more than a little paragraph, but it sums up everything I have to say. My hands shake as I fold it in half and write her name on the front. A tear drips from my eye and lands on the H of her name, smearing the ink. I'm not going to write it again. Forget it. I'll cry like a little fucking bitch and then decide not to leave.

I snatch my bag off the floor as I walk out. I know Reaper will see the cut and the letter when they have church in a few hours. It's cowardly leaving like this, in the middle of the night, not saying goodbye to everyone and facing the music like a man, but again, I wouldn't leave if I did that.

This is the only way.

I tiptoe past Pirate again and creep out the front door, the cold air hitting my face.

I'm not sure where I'm going, but I'll go 'til the blacktop ends or I run out of gas; until then, I'm going to ride.

CHAPTER ONE

Boomer

THE RIDE FROM SIN CITY LEADS ME TO AMERICA'S PLAYGROUND. Atlantic City, New Jersey just got a new resident. I've been riding for four days, stopping at mom and pop hotels along the highway, some more questionable than others, but I made it out alive, and now I'm on the East Coast.

Beach is to my left, casinos to my right, and I know if I'm not careful, I'm going to gamble every night until I hit it big. I need to be disciplined if I'm going to make it here. I rev my engine and speed up when the sign says I can go fifty-five instead of thirty-five. Hell yeah. There's nothing I love more than opening up the throttle and feeling the wind against my face.

My cheeks hurt from the sun, and my lips are a bit chapped from licking them, but it feels good. It's freeing. My head hurts from the damn helmet. I've worn it too much over the last few days, hours at a time, and I can't wait to get a hotel room, lean back, and relax. The one thing about being on a bike all day is the body starts to hurt, legs and back, and nothing sounds better than a hot bath and a nice jerk-off session to relax me.

Fuck yeah, that sounds good.

Just the thought has my dick twitching, and I don't know if it's actually from the anticipation of an orgasm or the vibration of the motor between my legs. It's been so long since I've gotten laid. The only thing I've been doing is jacking-off because the cut-sluts weren't doing it for me anymore.

Not going to lie, no female was. I wasn't getting hard. I secretly saw a therapist, and he said with all the other negative emotions I'm feeling, it's affecting my sex drive. I figure I'm just broken. A man who can't get it up for a woman isn't a man at all. Hell, I'm only twenty. I should be walking around with an erection and fucking everything in sight.

But it's the last thing on my mind. I just want to concentrate on me and get myself right, figure out who I am. I don't need to get pussy involved. Shit always gets fucking complicated when pussy is involved, and I don't need complicated right now. My mind is complicated enough. It's a battle zone all on its own.

I roll to a stop for a red light and look left. The ocean is never ending and the lingering smell of salt is in the air, making me inhale and exhale just like when I was in therapy. With a view like this, I'll never need to see a therapist again. The sand, the waves, the sun setting over the edge of the water paints the skies a dark red that reminds me of a dragon's breath plant.

Yeah, so what? I fucking like plants too. They're relaxing, and dragon's breath has a really cool fucking name. It's a deep red that gets lighter at the tips of the plant, mimicking what a dragon's fire would look like.

No one knows that about me, that I like plants or that I've

K.L. SAVAGE

been to therapy. Sarah doesn't even know how bad my mind gets. It's debilitating. When it gets really bad, I'd usually go out to the middle of the desert and blow shit up. Fire is the only thing that tends to calm me, and that's some pyromaniac shit.

My therapist said to push my negative thoughts into something positive instead, so he recommended plants. Something to keep me busy, to tend to and take care of. Since I didn't want anyone to know, I'd buy small plants and keep them in a certain part of the desert. They'll be fine now. I made sure to get native plants that would thrive in the sand. While it helped, I still had a dark urge to blow everything up; to see flames, to light matches, to hear the sizzle of a fuse, to feel the rumble of a grenade beneath my feet.

I have the urge to lay there in darkness and let the intrusive thoughts consume me, to take over me; the compulsion that makes me feel better is flames.

I inhale another deep breath, and the wind takes the opportunity to blow, cooling my heated face. This is home now. A new beginning. Maybe I'll be better here, mentally. Maybe it was the MC that had me fucked up. I'll be better now.

Yeah, that's the chant I said on repeat after blowing something up.

Maybe it's true. Maybe I will be better.

"Damn, longest fucking light of my life. What the fuck?" I look right to see if anyone is coming, debating if I want to risk running the red light. My luck there's a camera or some shit, and I'll get my license plate in the system. They'll send the ticket to Reaper since that's my home address, and then I'll be screwed because he will have a way to find me.

I'll sit and wait patiently.

A car rolls up next to me, an old convertible Volkswagen bug. It's light blue, a bit beat up, but the women in it sure are pretty.

"Hi." The driver giggles, flipping her long blonde hair over her shoulder while sucking on a blow pop. Seeing her tongue wrap around that candy should get me hard, but it doesn't. Nothing is happening below the belt. "Where you off to, handsome?" she purrs, turning her head back to tell her friend something, and then the blonde leans over the window, her black triangle bikini barely covering her tits. "Want to come back with us? We're only here for a night, and you look like you'd be a good time."

She has no idea what kind of man I am. Blondes usually aren't my thing, probably because my sister is blonde. Every time I see one, my dick shrivels up because I think of her. I'm into redheads, they're hot, but not like raven-haired beauties. Fuck, I love a woman with long dark hair, but I've never found one who really zapped me.

If I meet the right girl, maybe I can get my cock up for her. Maybe she'll be able to get through the bullshit in my head and let me feel human.

"Thanks, ladies, but I got a long ride ahead." Not really. I'm here. I just want to go the fuck to sleep.

She pouts, sticking out her bottom lip that's stained red from the sucker. "You do? We can give you a long ride. All three of us."

Too bad they're all fucking blondes.

"Sorry, ladies. Best of luck," I say as the light turns green. I tilt my head in a kind gesture and hit the throttle, letting my dad's Harley grumble in my wake. There are two things that sound right in this world: a loud bike and a woman screaming my name, and since I have one of those, I consider my life pretty fucking good.

I zip down the highway, a seagull flying next to me for a moment before I speed up and leave it behind. I rest one hand on my thigh, cruising at a decent speed so I can take in the view. Lights of the casinos strobe in the early night. People are coming out for a good time, hoping they'll hit it big at the casino.

It feels good. Something feels right about this place. I'm not sure what. I can't put my finger on it, but it's good, and I haven't felt good in a while. I come to another stop before I see a hotel right on the beach. Looks a little run down, probably has no a/c since some of the windows are open, but who needs air conditioning when the breeze from the ocean is right there? A bike stops next to me, a man in a leather cut, and he bows his head.

My heart pumps in my chest. No fucking way. When the light turns green, I let him pass by so I can get a good view of his cut. And right fucking there, it says Ruthless Kings, Jersey Chapter.

You have got to be kidding me. How the hell did I forget that? My palms start to sweat; no, you know what? It's fine. No one needs to know I'm here. My father was pretty well known through all the chapters, and his death was one that went down in history. If anyone finds out I'm here, they will roll out the red carpet, and I'm not trying to get involved in that.

I'll keep my distance and live my life away from them.

He gets further into the distance, and I watch him vanish into a small speck until I can't see him anymore. I want to make sure he doesn't turn around. Fuck, maybe I should go to another place. I don't want to be looking over my shoulder every five minutes.

When the sound of his bike is gone, I turn left and head

toward that little motel I saw before I got sidetracked with Ruthless Kings. Damn shit, it's going to follow me everywhere. I'm starting to wonder if it's a sign.

Gravel crunches under my tires when I pull into the parking lot of the ranch-style motel. It's small and old, with a red neon Motel sign that says Vacancy. I come to a slow stop, park, and cut the engine. I groan as I slide off my helmet. My hair is matted and stuck to my head from the sweat. I can't wait to get in that bathtub and relax. I run my fingers through my scalp and groan, then I turn my head left and right to pop my neck and nearly fall off my bike from how good it feels.

"Fuck me," I moan to the ground, taking a few deep breaths. My legs tingle from the blood flow rushing back to my weak feet when I stand. I take a few steps, stretch, and pop my back. I might be young, but damn it if I don't feel old.

I unhook my backpack from my bike and sling it over my shoulder. My boots crunch against the rocks, and I flick the flame of my lighter on and off, on and off. I love watching it light. The hedges around the motel are overgrown, the blue paint over the siding looks like it needs to be redone, and it's filthy. A few windows are broken, but the view can't be beat.

The ocean is right there.

The doorbell jingles when I open it, and just as I thought, the air is a bit sticky. The only thing recirculating it is an old fan that clicks with every spin above me. Other people wouldn't find this place amazing, but I find it charming, a diamond in the rough.

An old man comes to the window, clean silver hair combed back, dressed in corduroy pants and a white shirt. He has a beer belly, telling me he loves having a few longnecks before bed. I can understand that.

Me fucking too.

"One room?" he says through the thick plastic between us which makes him sound muted.

"Just the one," I reply. "Do you rent out rooms for apartments?" Might as well shoot my shot. I'm looking for a cheap place, a roof over my head; I don't care where.

"I do," he grumbles, wiping some crumbs off his mouth from the sandwich he just bit into. "It's a hundred a week. Place is run down; it's why I don't charge more. I'm not as fit as I used to be, and I can't fix half the shit wrong with this place. Take it or leave it," he says simply, on a bit of a huff.

"I'll take it, and I'll be glad to help. I can fix things up, and we can get this place looking good as new," I offer, wanting to do something decent for someone else. I have to start making friends somewhere, right?

"Really?" he asks. "What's the catch? I don't want no wild parties here. I see those tattoos on ya and that nose ring. You're a wild one, aren't ya? Oh, my Betsy would have loved you. God rest her soul; I don't know why she married me when she loved the bad boys."

"Ah, we get old. We're just temporary until a woman finds her true love," I say with a smile.

I thought he would laugh at my joke, but his eyes narrow at me, and his bottom jaw protrudes out further than his top, so when he frowns, he looks mean. "You listen here, there's someone for everyone, tattoos or not. I don't wanna hear that shit."

"Yes, sir," I say, trying not to smile. "We have a deal?"

He opens the door next to the window and steps out. He offers his hand to me. "We do. I'm Homer. Welcome to Oceanside Inn."

"Thank you. I'm Boomer. It's good to be here." I notice my slip as soon as I say it. I'm not Boomer anymore. I'm Jenkins, but I can't let the nickname go. It fits. It's the one thing that feels like *me*.

I glance at my phone after releasing Homer's hand and see that I have fifteen voicemails, a hundred texts, and dozens of missed calls. I know who they're from.

So I ignore them, put my phone away, and follow Homer to the room I'm going to rent. It's time to press the reset button on my life.

And it makes a pretty big boom, internally.

CHAPTER TWO

Scarlett

I DON'T KNOW WHERE I AM.

It's cold. It's dark. The ground is wet and hard, maybe cement? I know my wrists are bound, my ankles have something attached to them too, and by the rattle against the floor and the resistance when I move, I'm assuming shackles. I'm chained like a dog.

My head swims. I'm drowsy. I can't remember much. I lean back against the wall, and the rough concrete scratches against my shoulders. That's when I notice I'm not wearing a shirt or pants. The ground is rubbing my flesh raw and making it sore. My panties are chafing my inner thigh from all the moisture on the ground and in the air. I lean forward to try to explore my surroundings, but something around my neck stops me.

"What?" I say to myself, reaching my hand to touch whatever is stopping me from going two feet in front of me. My hand comes in contact with something hard and thick, and it's attached to another chain.

A collar.

I am a dog.

Tears burn my eyes from the horror I find myself in. I have no idea where I am. Who would do this to me? Why would someone do this? I'm confused, more than confused. I was on my way to my eight-a.m. class, and then I ... I don't remember.

I pull on the collar, yanking it, and hot tears fall down my face at my weak attempt.

"Don't bother."

I scream from the sudden, unexpected voice coming from the shadows. It's a woman. She sounds weak, like she's been here for a while. Her voice is dry, rough like sandpaper, and it makes my skin crawl with fear.

What's happened to her ... and will it happen to me?

"Hello? Who's there? Who are you?" I ask her, my voice echoing off the acoustic of the walls.

"Abigale."

"Abigale. I'm Scarlett. Do you know where we are? What's happening?" My throat tightens under the collar as I swallow, trying to coat my dry mouth. I can't be here. I've done everything right in my life. I've made good grades, dated good guys; I've only had sex once. I'm a good girl. I've done everything by the damn book. I don't deserve this.

"You don't remember anything either, huh?" Abigale's hoarse voice struggles to say. "You'll remember. You'll never forget this place or what these men will do to you. Welcome to the clubhouse of the Ruthless Kings. Where they are truly ruthless in what they do."

"What are you talking about? Who are the Ruthless Kings?" I question her. "Have there been others? How long have you been down here?"

"Few months, I think. I don't really know anymore. You lose track of time down here."

"A few… what?" My voice gets pitchy with panic, and a million terrible scenarios play in my head. "Abigale, please tell me what's going to happen. Please," I beg through hysterical tears, fear, the hopelessness I feel.

Her sigh is loud and full of exhaustion, not annoyance. "Ruthless Kings are a motorcycle club. There are good ones and bad ones—"

"This is a bad one. I'm going to go ahead and assume that."

"You'd be right," she says. "There used to be other girls here, but after they got their use out of them, depending on how they look, they sell them, or they kill them. I was the only one left for a while, until you."

"What do they do to you?" I whisper, picking my broken nail off. The anxiety of being in an unknown place, in the dark, talking to a voice in the shadows—which could be a ghost for all I know because I hit my head or something, and I'm losing it. Yep, completely losing it.

"What haven't they done? When they want me, they unchain me and use me up. I dance for them, and if I don't, there are consequences."

"Use you up? Consequences? Like what? Give me details! I need to know what's going to happen to me."

"They're going to pass you around, for one. Each and every single one of them are going to rape you. And don't fight them; they like it when you fight them. They will beat you if you don't dance. They get you high, and let me tell you, while you might not do drugs now, you'll be thankful. The drugs make everything numb. It makes what is happening to you easier."

"Easier?" I spit in shock. I can't believe she would say something like that. "Easier? Nothing could make this easier. How could you say that?"

"Because I've been here for months. I've lived this. You haven't. You'll see the reality. I'm sorry this is happening to you. Believe me—you'll wish for death. I do."

My heart grows cold, and the air freezes in my lungs like ice. I don't want to die. I don't want any of this. I have no idea what to do right now. How do I get free?

I don't reply to Abigale. What's there to say? My future has been delivered to me, and it's obviously meant for me to live in fear and misery.

"What did you do before this?" Abigale asks after too much silence. I finally hear her chains move, and the noise makes me relax. She's real. It isn't in my head. It's hard to decipher since it's so dark in here.

"I was a college student. I didn't have a major yet. I'm only twenty. I liked science, though. I thought of majoring in biology or something. Guess that's not happening anymore," I say more to myself. "What about you?"

"I was a nurse. I loved my job. I'm twenty-five. I'm sorry this happened to you so young," she says, and that makes me laugh to the point that I'm crying.

"I'm sorry. I don't mean to laugh. I guess I don't know what else to do. I'm young? You're young too, Abigale. You're just starting the life you worked so hard to build."

"I know," she says. "And I understand. Sometimes laughter

is better than the tears. Your new reality sucks. This fucking sucks, and it's scary. I want you to know it's okay to be scared, but I'm telling you right now, don't let them see your fear. Pretend as though you like what they're doing to you, and it stops a hell of a lot sooner because they like their girls to fight them. Okay? I'm not sure how much longer I'll be around. Girls don't usually make it this long. I'm sorry for the harshness of it all. There's no way to pretty it up, and I'm not going to give you hope because that's cruel. There's no hope here. There is no pretty."

I like that she's telling me the truth. It prepares me, somehow, even if I think no one can prepare me at all for what's about to happen."

"There's this one guy. I don't know his name. He's nicer than the others. He brings food and water and hangs out for a bit to talk, brings a light too. He doesn't have sex with the girls. He makes sure he isn't around when they rape us. I asked him why he can't help or do more to protect us, but he's a victim too. His "brothers" use his sister as leverage against him if he doesn't comply with their every wish."

"God, that's terrible." But that's hope. If we can get him to release us—

"I know what you're thinking. No. I've tried. He caught on, and he said he hates what he knows, but his sister comes first. It's his own family."

"That's a tough spot to be in." To do nothing. That doesn't make him a good guy. "Surely, he could do something, and the fact that he chooses not to is wrong, and his sister would be disappointed.

"He's tried to free girls before, and guess what? They killed his mom right in front of him, after they beat her. So yeah, he won't go against them again. His sister is the only family he has left."

"Jesus," this gets darker and darker by the second. Who does such a thing? "Why can't he leave the club?"

"The only way out of the club is death, so he says, and he refuses to die because then no one can protect his sister."

"There has to be something he can do," I say on a whine. "Anything." I have never sounded so small in my entire life, but what else do I do? Being brave or courageous doesn't seem to matter right now. Nothing I do will guarantee my survival. I'm leashed. They are in control of me.

"Maybe. Whatever it is, he hasn't figured out a way yet. He's just a foot soldier. He isn't a ranking member."

"You sure do know a lot about the man for not knowing his name."

"Well, when you're here alone, you tend to beg for anything, so I begged for his company," she snorts. "Can you believe that? I begged for the company of a man who belongs to a club like this."

"Sounds like he doesn't like it either."

"Doesn't really matter, does it? Our fate is sealed." She coughs an awful wet cough, one that requires the care of a doctor.

"You sound really sick, Abigale. Are you okay?"

"I'm fine. It's just an upper respiratory thing."

Yeah, I don't believe her. The cough is deep, in her lungs and chest. She needs medicine. I only know because I had pneumonia last year, and it sounded just like that. "Maybe that man who comes down can help? He can bring you medicine if we tell him."

"I don't want to get him in trouble," she says.

"I will," I nearly growl. Who cares? My life is ruined anyway. I might as well piss a few bikers off along the way. What are they going to do that I don't already expect?

A loud thud bangs, and I gasp, tilting my head up to see where the noise is coming from.

"Don't say a word," Abigale whispers. "They're back."

I scurry against the wall again, pressing my back so far into it that I feel the rock cutting my skin, but I don't care. I want the wall to swallow me up and hide me away. The first thud of footsteps above hit the floor, and sand and dust fall, getting into my eyes. I blink it away and rub my face. My eyes water from the intrusion.

One pair of boots turn into another, then another, and then it sounds like a stampede. They're laughing, a loud roar that can be heard for miles, but under it, there's screaming, crying.

They have another girl.

"Oh, no," Abigale says at the same time. She must hear it too.

"Shut up," one of the deep biker's voice yells, and then a loud slap makes me cover my mouth to keep me from screaming. "Shut the fuck up, you slut," he says.

"Please, don't do this," the girl begs him. "Please, my father. He has a lot of money—"

"We're counting on it," the biker cackles, and the basement door opens, allowing light in. I wince, my eyes not ready for the harsh brightness. I hold my hand above my eyes to try to block it out. "Wolf, take her down there."

"Yes, Prez."

"And then feed them and shit."

The boots coming down the steps are slow.

Bang.

Bang.

Bang.

I see a faint shadow of the man. He's big, broad, and that's all I can tell. The basement is still too dark.

"I'm sorry," he says to the girl. "I really am." His voice catches, like he cares or is getting emotional, but I don't believe it for a second. He might have given the sad story to Abigale, but I don't buy it. He's probably playing her.

"I'm begging you," the girl pleads, the innocence clear as day. "Please." Her sobs break my heart, and it's then I'm thankful that I was drugged. I didn't have to feel the fear on the way over. Maybe Abigale is right; maybe the drugs are the answer to get through this entire ordeal until the course of my life changes… if it changes.

And right now, I'm not too sure if I want life at all because the memories will be all I have.

CHAPTER THREE

Boomer

MY FIRST NIGHT SPENT IN THE RUNDOWN MOTEL WENT smoothly; well, as smooth as someone can expect in a place like this. The yellow shag carpet is from the seventies and kind of smells like weed. The TV is one of those boxed ones, and I can't help but wonder if that shit is still in black and white. I haven't turned it on. It's like stepping into a time machine. If Homer wants to redo this place, he needs to redo everything and not just the outside.

My back hurts too. The mattress is lumpy as fuck, which probably hasn't been changed since he built this place. And I don't want to think about that because it grosses me out that I've been laying on a bed that has been there since before I was born.

The bathroom, fucking hell, the bathroom is this ugly olive-green color, and the floor is yellow. I'm hoping it's the color of the tile and not the buildup of piss over the years. It doesn't smell like piss, so that says something.

I open the window to allow the sea breeze in to circulate the stuffy room. I do have a small patio, just fifty yards away from the ocean. It's overgrown with weeds, and the chairs look like they used to be white. One of the legs is broken, and it's leaning against the rotten wood that makes up the railing.

I place my elbows on the porch railing, and the slight give of my weight causes it to creak, but I catch myself when I feel my body going with it. Half of the railing falls into the sand, and I shake my head, running my fingers through my dirty blond hair that's a bit too long. I need to cut it.

The ocean breeze hits me, that salt sticking to my shirtless skin, and goose bumps arise all over me. It's cold right now. It's early morning, and the sun has barely peeked over the edge of the water. I love watching the sun rise. It makes me feel like I'm living instead of missing out on everything beautiful.

"Hey, kid," Homer says, hobbling over from a few rooms down.

My heart skips from the nickname. Reaper used to call me that, still does every now and then. He forgets I'm grown, but I guess when I'm younger than everyone around me, they'll look at me like a kid.

"Homer, what are you doing up? It's only five," I say, glancing at my watch.

"Sleep is for the dead, and I may look it, but I'm not. Don't give me any shit about it. We need to talk about work around here."

"Alright. Let me go put a shirt on, and you and I can go for some breakfast. How about that?"

"Fine, but you're buying. I got a business to run," he

huffs. "I'll be up front. Half-naked, tatted troublemaker," he mumbles as he walks away. "What have I gotten myself into? He seems like a good kid." He's talking to himself, debating what to do about me.

I chuckle and step inside my room and rummage through my backpack for a clean white t-shirt. I like Homer. He's a cranky son of a bitch, but I like that about him. He doesn't seem to take shit from people, and I respect that. He's alone too, and an old man being on his own bothers the shit out of me.

I snag my wallet and room key off the small table by the window, then shut and lock the door behind me. My boots sink in the sand as I make my way through the tunnel to the office. It's open to the sand and breeze and sound of the ocean. Homer leans against the wall, cigarette hanging from his mouth.

"Took you fucking long enough," he gripes, flicking the ashes off the glowing tobacco. "I ain't getting any younger, kid."

"Obviously, you're old as dirt," I say with a smile, and he shakes his fist at me, that damn underbite giving him a fearsome, but adorable old man look.

"I might look old, but I have the heart of a lion, and I'm not afraid to bite!"

"That I don't doubt, Homer." I slap his back and take the keys from him. "What do you drive?"

"That old Bronco, but I can drive. I'm not inept yet."

"If I let you drive, we'll never get there. I see how old people are on the road, peeking over the wheel, hunkered over like they can't see three-feet in front of them and, Homer, no offense, but I'm hungry and need coffee."

He huffs, scurrying his feet along the pavement. The blue cardigan is the same one he wore yesterday along with the pants. He opens the passenger-side door and hops in without help. He peeks his balding head out the window, mean-mugging me before slamming the door.

I whistle, not bothering to look at him as I step up into the old, rusted Bronco. Damn, this thing would be a beauty with some TLC.

"I didn't want to drive anyway," he mutters next to me as I put the vehicle in drive.

"Right, I know you didn't, Homer." My lips tilt in a smirk, and I pull out of the parking lot to get onto the road. "So where are we headed? I'm new to town, remember?"

"Right, right. What brings you here anyway? No… I don't want to know. Not right now. You can tell me over coffee actually. I'm sure it's something scandalous. Let's go to Cherry's. They have good pie. You're going to want to take a left at the next light, then the next right, and then it will be right there. You can't miss it. If you miss it, you're a fucking idiot. I knew I should've drove."

"Damn, way to give a guy a chance, Homer. You wound me." I place my hand over my heart, faking that I give a shit.

"Hootenanny! I damn well doubt anything could hurt you," he says. "I've seen your type before. All big and bad."

"You're wrong," I tsk. Plenty bothers me, like the fear that I'm slowly going crazy, and one day I'll be in a straitjacket in a padded room.

"I'm never wrong," Homer says. "I was only ever wrong with my Betsy."

"How the hell she dealt with you, I'll never know. She's a saint for putting up with your cranky ass."

"Boy," he laughs, slapping his knee. "Don't I know it? She was an angel." Homer practically sighs. I take that right he bitched about, and I steal a glance to see him dabbing his eyes with a napkin. "Damn, allergies."

"Yeah, they suck, don't they?" I know damn good and well he's crying cause he misses his late wife. Hell, I hope one day I find love. I want someone to bring me out of the darkness I find myself living in, someone who will deal with me on my bad days because I fucking have a shit-ton of bad days. It's hard to find something to live for when the shadow inside grips me, trying to bring me under.

Sometimes I want to give in, but something stops me. I can't put my finger on it, but it's enough for me to not walk into the ocean right now and let the waves take me. Hell, maybe I'm meant to be here, with Homer, fixing up his motel. I believe everything happens for a reason, and right now, I'm just trying to figure out what that reason is.

We pull into the paved parking lot of Cherry's, the sign a big cherry pie. In old black letters against a white backing it says, "A free piece of pie if you say hi."

"Well damn, looks like I'm saying hi," I say.

"They're true to their word too," Homer replies, swinging the door open. He didn't have trouble getting up in the Bronco, but he can't seem to get down. He grunts and curses, holding on to the 'oh shit' handle to help himself down.

I don't want him to hurt himself. I'm not a heartless bastard like a lot of people think; people being the Ruthless Kings—my brotherhood. What used to be my brotherhood. I hurry around the Bronco to help the old geezer down, but he slaps my hands away.

"Hey, I don't need help. I can do this on my own." He

turns red-faced as he continues to try, and the more he tries, the more I want to help him. I don't like seeing people suffer. Well, wait … that isn't true. I like to see people who deserve to suffer, suffer. Just like Sarah's abuser. I enjoyed what I did to him. Fucking hell, I get excited just thinking about putting that grenade in his mouth and watching the house go *boom*.

"Alright, enough of this." I put my hands under his armpits and pick him up, then place him right on his feet. "Listen here, Homer, I'm not about to watch you struggle when I can help. You might think I'm some thug, popping caps or some bullshit, but whatever you think I do, I don't." Not really. He doesn't need to know facts. "And the way I see it, you're going to be seeing a lot of me. Probably until the day you die, so tough fucking titty. I'm going to help. And you can just be grouchy about it for all I care."

"Fine," he spits, shuffling by me.

I expected more of a fight. "Well, come on; coffee ain't gonna pour itself. Let's go," he shouts, but he's only two of my strides ahead of me since he's hunched over and sliding dirt with his shoes with every step.

I follow behind him and hear a roar of motorcycles in the distance. I stop and look over my shoulder. My palms sweat. It's them. I know it. Only men who are in a club have bikes that sound like that.

"You coming? Good lord, and I thought I was as slow as dirt." Homer opens the front door, and the little bell jingles as he enters.

The bikes come to view, and I turn away quickly, hurrying after Homer. I need to put the MC behind me, but wherever I go, they're right there, even if they aren't my chapter. The door closes behind me, and a few people look in my direction and then look away. A man at the counter sips his coffee, and the waitress behind the bar has two high ponytails, chewing bubblegum as she takes someone's order.

I look around for Homer and see him in the back, settling in a corner booth. I make my way over the black and white checkered tiles. The booths are a bright red, and the tables are silver. It's a classic-looking diner, and it smells fucking great in here; like pie right out of the oven.

A few women look my way. I feel their eyes on me. I'm a big guy, and the tattoos give me a bad boy appeal. Women seem to always have a kink for it, but I'm not looking to be anyone's kink. I've done that, been doing that since I was fifteen and knew what sex was. It's old.

I plop down in the booth, and Homer takes a menu from the holder against the wall. I do the same, reaching behind the ketchup, mustard, syrup, and other condiments.

The roar of the motorcycles come into the parking lot, and the engines rumble to silence. I do my best not to show distress. I swear to god, if they notice me somehow, I'm going to be pissed. I'll have to up and leave again, and I don't want to do that. I like it here. I like Homer's cranky ass.

"Hi, welcome to Cherry's. I'm Sylvia, and I'll be your waitress this early morning. Can I start you off with some coffee?"

"Hi there, Sylvia," Homer croons kindly, a side of him I haven't seen before. I hide my face behind the menu and grin. "Do I still get my pie?" He makes his voice sound older and more decrepit.

The old man is milking it.

"Of course, you do! Oh my goodness, aren't you just adorable," the waitress exclaims, writing down on her notepad.

"Hi," I greet. "I'd like some coffee too, black."

"Sure thing. And what kind of pie do you want, handsome?" she bites her pink-painted bottom lip and eyes me up.

Yep, she has the kink too.

"You have apple?" I ask, glancing away from her green eyes and dirty blond hair to look at the menu. The ribeye and eggs look good. I could go for some steak.

"Sure do. Be back in a jiffy," she winks at me.

Homer watches her go, and when he looks at me again, he clicks his tongue. "I think she likes you."

"All the girls do. They see a bad boy, but then they get the bad, and they don't like it so much."

"Well, you don't seem so bad to me," Homer barely says, as if it hurts for him to say.

"Homer, you don't know anything about me. You hired a stranger to do your work."

"I know, but I have a good feeling about you," he says just as the waitress comes over and fills our mugs with coffee.

"Oh, that smells good," I groan. I'm more awake now, just from the scent of coffee.

"I brewed a fresh pot just for you handsome fellas." She eyes me again, and I shift in my seat, feeling a bit uncomfortable. I never used to be like this. I hate the person I am.

Do something about it. There's a way to make it better.

The thoughts in my head speak up, and I clench my hands tighter around the mug, letting the heat soak into my palms. The doorbell jingles, and the waitress, who's all happy and smiles, looks over her shoulder to see the bikers come in, and a frown quickly replaces the joy. The air shifts with something dark, dangerous, and a hint of fear is in the air. They sit in the booth behind us, and I look at Homer to see him eyeing the men behind me.

"What are we going to do with the girls?" one of them says to the other, low and deep. They don't think anyone can hear them. Are they fucking nuts? And what girls? What's this chapter doing that's making the Ruthless King name bad? I'm not getting a good feeling.

No, I need to stay out of this. New start. New me.

"What we always do. Now shut up and look at the menu."

That must be the Prez.

"And when we're done, we're going to fuck those fine ass girls in the basement, sell them, and maybe buy a new bike or two," the Prez whispers to his men.

Just what the fuck is going on in this city? Homer knows something by how he's looking at his coffee and not at me.

And I plan to figure it out.

CHAPTER FOUR

Scarlett

"**H**EY, WAKE UP." I groan, not wanting to wake up. Every day is night, and I can't tell when I should stay awake or sleep.

"I have water and food. Come on, girl. Wake up." A hand jostles me, and I snap my eyes open, ready to fight for my damn life, but I see two hands instead of a face with a faint glow of a lamp behind him.

My eyes adjust to the weak light. It's been days of darkness, but somehow, I'm still here, untouched, along with a few others. There's Abigale, Joanna, and Melissa. Melissa came earlier, and now that there are more of us, I worry for Abigale since she's been here the longest.

A face finally focuses in my vision; the man is young with wild hair and a nose ring. He is handsome. It's too bad he's a piece of shit. Most good-looking guys aren't worth nothing, so my late grandma said.

"It's okay, Scarlett. It's him. It's the guy I told you about," Abigale says.

"You're Wolf," I croak. I half expect dust to fall from my lips.

"How do you know my name?" he asks. He doesn't sound mad, just surprised. He's younger than I expected. His voice is smoother, and his eyes aren't full of hatred, just pure sadness and regret.

"I heard one of the guys call you that when they opened the door," I explain. "Water?"

"Yeah, here." He unscrews the cap and places the plastic bottle in my hands. I bring it to my cracked, bleeding lips and drink the gold down, letting it coat my throat. "Don't drink it all. You need to eat. I brought everyone a sandwich and some chips. I know it isn't much, but it's all I can do today."

I haven't eaten in days because I've chosen not to, but when the smell of roast beef hits my nose, my stomach grumbles. I launch forward like I'm some sort of animal, ripping the sandwich apart with my hands. I whimper, crying as I stuff my face. I hate that I've become this. This inhuman thing chained to a wall, eating like a barbarian, but it's all I can do.

It's all I am now.

I chug the rest of the water down and then throw the empty bottle at Wolf's face. "You should be used to taking out the trash. Next, it will be us, right?" I wipe my mouth against my arm and wince when I taste dirt and salt from my sweat.

"It isn't like that. I don't view you as trash." He sounds hurt. He leans back on his legs and rubs his hands over his face, exhaling heavily. "I'm doing what I have to."

"So I've heard. Maybe you aren't doing enough," I hiss. "You obviously care. Look at us," I shout at him, the word breaking on a sob. "Look at me. They are going to kill me, or worse. I have a life. I've worked hard. I have a family. I have goals. Please don't do this."

His eyes water. Or, at least, I think they do. I can't tell if it's the trick of the light or not. He falls to his ass and lays his elbows on his knees. "You don't think I know that? That I don't think about you women down here every second of every day? You don't think it eats me up inside? It does. I'm fucked. I don't want to be here. I'm only here because my father was a member, and I was forced to be one. The one time I stepped out of line, they killed my mother in front of me, so yeah, I do as I'm told to now. You better fucking believe it." He takes out a cigarette, lights it with a Zippo lighter, and the glow of the ember creates a small sun as he sucks in. Wolf blows out the thick cloud of smoke, and I inhale the secondhand, hoping it seeps into my lungs. I'm not a smoker, but I wouldn't mind something to ease the tension I feel.

"I care, okay? I don't want you guys down here. Be glad it's me who comes down and not one of the other assholes."

"Why do you care?" I ask, sniffling, and the other girls do the same. Their distress, while contained, is loud to me.

"Because hurting people, hurting women, isn't something I do. I don't like it. I can't get out of the club or they'll hurt Rayleen. I won't let that happen. I'd rather be damned for life, if it means she'll have a good life."

"And you're okay with damning us too?" I say in a low whisper, playing with the bottle cap on the floor. I definitely feel damned. I feel chained by the hands of the devil, waiting to drag me to hell.

"No, I'm not. I'm doing what I can. I'm thinking. I can't let them on to it. Just I'm trying, okay?"

Abigale wheezes, barely able to catch a breath.

"Listen, she's sick. She needs a doctor or medicine. Can't you get something? What if it spreads to us? I'm sure your boss or whoever it is won't like that."

His eyes flash knowingly, because I'm right. "I can get something."

"Thank you," I say.

"Don't ever thank me. I don't deserve it. When they come back from their run, they're going to take one of you, and I'm going to have to watch them do whatever it is they want to do. I'm going to be sick about it. I'll want to pull out my gun and kill them, but I'd die and then my sister won't have anyone, and neither will you all. Just don't ever fucking thank me."

He gives me his back and goes to Abigale, touching her forehead with the back of his hand. Her face glistens with sweat, and she's pale, clammy. "If they see her like this, they'll get rid of her."

"What if you did?" I say with realization.

"What are you talking about?" he asks, peeking over his shoulder, his gold nose ring gleaming in the light.

"What if you get rid of her because she's really sick. You say you killed her, but you take her somewhere. Right? You can do that. You know… you had to do it to protect the club or something." Hope. The thing that Abigale warned me about blooms in my chest like a flower. This is it. This is the chance we need to let someone know we're here.

He turns around, the sole of his shoe still on the floor, and his brows pinch together. He's deep in thought. Wolf looks back at Abigale and shakes his head. "I don't know how it will work. They won't believe me."

"Shoot her. In the shoulder. They'll see the blood; they'll have proof," I say, hating that I just tossed Abigale under the bus like that, but if she gets out, she can save us all, and she can heal.

"Do it," Abigale says. "Whatever I have, it's killing me. I need a doctor anyway," she wheezes. "It's pneumonia, I think." She takes another breath, and her effort just to get air is shaky. "Get rid of me. You only have a few hours, Wolf."

"Abigale…" His voice breaks as he cups her face, as if he truly cares about her. "I can't. I can't shoot you."

He's grown attached to her.

"You," she wheezes, "have to."

"I can't do that with the rest of you. They won't believe me."

"I know," I reply, getting to my raw, aching knees. I stumble over when the collar jerks me back. "I know, but anything will help. If you care at all, this is the way to our freedom. She's sick, and she's going to die if you don't get her help. They know she's sick, right? It's why they haven't been down here."

He nods, smoothing his hand over his face in a stressful gesture. Wolf stands and starts to pace, caging his head in with his arms by lacing his hands behind his neck. "Fuck, I'll be in trouble if I do this and get caught."

"You won't," Abigale wheezes and reaches out for his hand. "I wouldn't ever do anything to put you in jeopardy, Wolf. You've made my time here bearable."

He falls to his knees and lays his head against hers. "I'm sorry. I'm so sorry I couldn't help you more. When you get out of here, you're going to do good in life, okay? Promise me."

"Wolf—"

I glance away from their private moment. I'm not too sure how Abigale can love one of them, even if he does seem better than the rest. I understand he's in a tough spot, and maybe he hasn't had the chance to get rid of one of us until now, or he hasn't thought of this idea. Whatever the reason, it isn't enough for me. Nothing will be enough for me to ever like any man who wears a cut, who rides a damn bike, who wears boots. I'm fucking done with men if I make it out of this.

How Abigale can even look at Wolf, I will truly be forever baffled.

"It's going to hurt," Wolf says. He reaches into his cut, the one with the skull wearing a crown on the back and pulls out a large gun. The barrel is long, silver, and the handle is ivory, I think, since it has a shine to it. "It's going to burn, you're going to bleed, and you're going to cry. It's like fire spreading through your entire body. The pain only ever ends if you bleed out enough or you get help. That's it." Wolf points the gun at her shoulder and cocks the hammer.

The bullet entering the chamber makes me hold my breath. There isn't a sound like it, the glide of metal against metal as the promise of pain or death rings through the air. Abigale stares at Wolf, wheezing, tears falling to her cheeks. "I love you," she says. "You're the only thing about this place I love."

"Don't say that to me." He points the gun away. "You can't say shit like that to me. I don't fucking deserve it. I don't deserve your love."

He doesn't, but Abigale gave it anyway.

She wraps her hand around the barrel and takes the gun from him. "You do. You deserve more than this place. You're more than this place, Wolf." She coughs and turns the gun on herself, pointing it at her shoulder. "I shouldn't have asked you to do this. It wasn't fair."

"I can do it. I'll do it," Wolf says. "If you want me to."

She cries, shaking her head. "I don't know if I can pull the trigger."

Wolf wraps his hands around hers, laying his finger on the trigger. "We'll do it together, okay?"

"Okay. Okay." She coughs and spits up blood. "That's not good. If we're gonna do this, we need to do it now."

Wolf leans down and says something in her ear, and by the slight smile on her face, I'm assuming he declared his love. He stays there, hunched over to be close to her. And barely, just barely, I hear him count down.

One.

Two.

Three.

The gunshot is as loud as Abigale's screams. My ears ring. I can't hear anything. I watch as Wolf swings her up into his arms. Blood trickles down her arms, spreading across her chest as the red liquid leaks from the hole in her body.

Wolf runs up the steps, and we're left in silence.

I just got a woman shot.

Holy shit, what have I done? It will be worth it, right? I had to do what I had to do to live. Abigale was on board; she said so.

I hear Wolf's countdown in my head, repeating. One, two, three, one, two, three. I can't help but think I signed Abigale's death warrant. And that feeling of not caring what happens to me starts to sink in.

One, two, three, one, two, three.

CHAPTER FIVE

Boomer

"**A**LRIGHT, OLD MAN. SPILL. WHAT'S GOING ON WITH those bikers?"

"Who you calling old? I could still beat your ass," Homer grunts.

I pull into the parking lot of the motel and turn, one arm stretched out behind the passenger seat and the other on the wheel. "Whatever you need to tell yourself, Homer. What's with those bikers?" I need to know everything about them. They spoke about women as if they have captives—selling them into sex trafficking, and it isn't right. They're up to no good. Ruthless Kings Vegas toe the line of the law, but it's completely against club bylaws to commit crimes against women or children. That shit is punishable to the highest offense by the club, and Reaper sure as shit didn't get his road name because he's a flowery fucker either. It's trouble. If I have to, I'll call Reaper and hope like hell he believes me. It's punishable to accuse another chapter of a crime, but since I'm not even a prospect anymore, hopefully I'd be in the clear. I just need proof.

"We don't talk about the Ruthless Kings. Not here." He looks to the left toward the beach and sighs, shoulders sagging. "This place, it used to be the place to come to. Tourists from all around the world would come here. My motel would be booked with college kids. They didn't care what the place looked like when they crashed. They needed to save money but enjoy spring break."

"What happened? Was it the Kings?" I ask again, trying to get some sort of information out of Homer.

"We don't talk about them, kid." He opens the door to get out, but I grab his arm, pulling him back in.

"I'm talking about them, Homer. Tell me what I need to know. Maybe I can help."

He laughs, shaking his head. His glasses fall to the tip of his nose, and the back of his hair sticks up from rubbing against the headrest. "What can you do against a bunch of bikers?"

If he only knew how fucked in the head I am. My reach goes farther than he thinks. "Just humor me, would you?" I say, slightly annoyed that I have to keep asking. How scary are these bikers? I've seen my fair share of fucked up shit, so if Homer is scared and if the town is scared, the bikers aren't doing what they need to do. They are supposed to protect the city, keep it safe, love it, not fill it with fear.

I squeeze the steering wheel with both hands and take a deep breath in through my nose and out through my mouth.

Homer leans forward and looks out the windshield, staring

at the old motel that used to be something. "I remember when this place was amazing. The day it stopped being amazing was when the Ruthless Kings came to town. They wanted money from me and my Betsy. They wanted in on all the hotels in Atlantic City. Hell, we weren't but in our thirties. We told them we didn't make much, but they didn't care. They threatened us if we didn't pay, threatened my Betsey."

I don't want him to continue because I have a bad feeling I know where this is going.

"I don't have the money to repair the inn because the Ruthless Kings take the majority of it. Hell, I can't even afford a home. I live here. They drain me. And the one time I missed a payment because we made no money, they killed my Betsey right in front of me. She was pregnant, you know. We never thought we would have kids. It was a miracle, especially at her age. She was thirty–seven, so it wasn't impossible, but we had been together twelve years and tried every single day. Damn, I was a dog. I don't know how she put up with me." Homer laughs and it quickly turns into a sniffle. "She was finally pregnant," he says. "And they took her from me. So I haven't missed a payment since, not that I have anything to live for, but what am I going to do? It's all I have left of what Betsy and I built together." Homer turns to me, his wrinkled face aging so much more in this moment than all the others I've known him for. "They are bad men, kid. They are no good. You're good," he hit my chest with his fist. "Don't get involved with them. They will ruin you."

It isn't fair that these men are taking advantage of so many people. Homer should be retired, living the good life, and maybe getting some old pussy to live out the remainder of his years as a king. "I don't want this life for you, Homer. You deserve better. The people of this city deserve better."

"It's life," he says. "It's how it is. You'll see when you're older."

I've seen enough and I'm only twenty. I want to tell him the truth about me, but it will only make him fear me. I don't want that. He is warming up to me and I can protect him from this. I can fix this. Maybe I can go to the clubhouse here and tell them to back the fuck off.

"Homer, they were talking about women. Where I am from, we don't hurt women. Do you know anything about that?"

He shakes his head. "No, they're a loud, reckless, bunch of drunks, but they keep business to themselves. I don't know anything about them except they are trouble. Why are you so interested?" His eyes narrow at me, assessing me.

"I'm just curious, is all. I want to know the kind of city I'm moving into." The entire point of this move was to start over, and I'm fucking lying.

"You moved to a city run by biker thugs. That's about all I can tell you."

Oh, I want to laugh so much right now, but it is not the right moment.

"Homer?" I gain his attention before he tries to get out of the car again.

"Yeah?"

"I'm sorry about your wife and your child. No man should have to go through that." I mean that. If the love of my life was ever taken from me like that, I think I'd probably kill myself. Homer is more of a man than I'll ever be. Living a life without love, hell it scares me enough, but to live a life and have loved only for it to be stolen from you?

That fucking terrifies me.

His hand pats my shoulder, and that's when I notice his wedding ring. It's old and dull. He probably hasn't taken it off since he put it on for the first time all those years ago. "Thanks, kid. I appreciate it. I hope you never have to deal with that in your life. You're young. You still have so much beauty to see. There is more to life than the hateful crimes of some gang."

"You going to tell me about her?" I ask as I open the driver's side door and hop out. My boots hit against the gravel, and when I look down, I see my father's boots, the ones that rode with his club for so many years. I know he would be disappointed in me right now, but I hope he understands if he is looking down on me.

I run around the front of the Bronco and open the door a bit wider to get to Homer. I lift him up and place him on the ground like I did before. He huffs and brushes his cardigan off. "Not a chance in hell. I don't know you well enough to tell you about my Betsy."

"Damn, I bet she was hot," I say, jabbing him a bit.

He shuffles his feet through the gravel, his back hunched over and curved. He almost looks like he needs a cane. "Hell yeah she was. She was the prettiest woman on the entire East Coast!"

"Just the East? I bet she'd be in shock you'd say such a thing," I tease, and in three strides I'm at his side, handing him the keys to his Bronco.

"Ah, hootenanny!" He brushes me off. "You sound just like she did. The East Coast can't be good enough? She needed all the damn directions. Woman bugged me until I admitted she was the prettiest in the world, and she was. She really was."

Hearing the forlornness in his voice stabs my heart. It isn't fair that a guy like Homer has had to live alone for so long, just as he started his life when she was taken from him. My goal is to make his life a little better, and in return, I hope my life gets better too.

We take a left around the corner, and my bike sits in the same spot as it did yesterday. The yellow gleams in the light, and the shining black reminds me of midnight. Homer stops and takes a look, whistling as he circles her.

That's right, her. A bike is all fine lines and curves, a sweet engine that purrs when you hit the throttle just right, which gives the bike the rightful title of *her*. Nothing better than a beautiful woman, and there is nothing better than a beautiful bike.

"That's a pretty piece of metal you got there, kid."

"Thanks. She belonged to my dad…" I run my finger over the matte black handlebars, nostalgia taking over me when the sudden knowledge hits me that my dad used to grab onto these same handles.

"Sorry to hear that." He offers me his condolences, not because the bike is mine, but the reason I have the bike in the first place.

"Thanks, Homer."

"Let's go inside and make a cup of coffee. All this heavy shit we keep talking about is giving me a headache. We can talk about what kind of repairs you want to do. I've been meaning to install some a/c—"

"No, Homer. You don't want that right now. It's nearly fall, and the weather is about to turn cold. Plus, the beach breeze is amazing. I think you should paint the outside first, clean it up."

We take a left into the dark tunnel that leads to his office, and Homer nods as he gets the key ring out that's attached to his belt.

"Help me."

"What did you say, Homer?" I ask him, looking around to see where the voice is coming from.

"I thought you said something," he says.

"Please," a small feminine voice, weak and raspy, calls out further into the tunnel.

"Stay here, Homer." I charge down the tunnel and even though the sun is out, with the location of the hallway, the light doesn't shine too far, and it leaves the majority of it in the dark.

"I'll be damn. Someone is hurt and needs help. I'm coming—" he grumps, and the sound of his feet sliding against the concrete make my lips tilt in the smallest grin. I think I'm starting to like the sound.

"Hello?" I call out.

"Help," she says again.

I take out my phone when I see a figure sitting by the utility closet and turn on the flashlight to see a woman sitting there against the door, bleeding profusely out of her shoulder. She's pale, sweaty, and looks like she hasn't had a shower in a few months. "Holy shit." I drop down on my knees next to her, and she immediately starts to cry. "It's okay. You're safe. You're safe here."

"Oh my god. I'm going to go call an ambulance," Homer says.

"No!" she shouts as loud as she can. "Please, no ambulances. No, they will find me if you do that. Please, help me. Please!" She grips my hand as tight as she can, staring at me through big blue eyes that are darkened with exhaustion. "I'll do anything," she begs. "Just don't make me have sex—"

"Woah, hey, hey." I cup her face gently, showing her some kindness. "We aren't those kind of men. You're safe." I slide my arms under her and lift, holding her small body against my chest. "I'm taking her to my room. Can you get some clean clothes or something, Homer? A first-aid kit?" I lean in closer and listen to her shaky breathing. "She might need some antibiotics too with how her breathing sounds. Lady, you need a doctor."

"No, please. No, doctors. Can't go to the hospital." She wheezes. "Scarlett. Need to get the girls. Save them."

"I'll be back in a jiffy," Homer says, scurrying those damn feet along the ground, but he's hurrying; I'll give him that.

She's speaking in broken sentences, but the name Scarlett resounds in me. I'm not sure what it is, but it feels familiar, even if I've never heard the name before. *It's just because there are other women. That's it. Other people need to be saved.*

"Ruthless Kings."

It's the last thing she says before passing out limp in my arms. I grit my teeth. Those fuckers are in for a rude awakening if they think for one fucking minute they can get away with this bullshit.

I'm going to blow them to pieces. One by fucking one.

And I'm going to enjoy every damn bloody, brutal, grotesque bit of it.

CHAPTER SIX

Scarlett

I'M NOT SURE HOW MANY DAYS IT'S BEEN SINCE ABIGALE LEFT. THE days are blending to one now. A never-ending hourglass with that sand that doesn't seem to ever stop. I've cried so much and so hard; I have no more tears left. Wolf only comes down to give us water and food, and then he leaves again. He doesn't stay like he used to.

He misses Abigale.

One of the other girls has a cough now, and it's only a matter of time before we all get sick. I'm going to die down here in this damn hole, and no one will ever know what happened to me. Abigale was our last chance of being rescued, and since nothing has happened, I'm going to assume the worst, just like Wolf is.

At least, that's why I think he hasn't stayed down here with us. Since we're still here, Abigale must have died.

I hit my head against the stone and whimper when the collar around my neck rubs against my raw skin.

Boots sound up above, and I freeze. They're slower than usual, and two deep voices, one belonging to Wolf, start to speak. I can't tell what they're saying because the voices are so drawn out and muted by the walls and floor between me and them.

The door to the basement groans, and fear bubbles in my chest just like every other time the damn thing opens.

Boom.

Boom.

Boom.

The sound of boots march to my impending death.

The light above flickers on for the first time since I've been here, and all the girls whimper in fear. I lift my cuffed hands to my face to block out the light, turning my back to try to get away from the harshness of it.

"Shit, I'm sorry. Fuck. I can be an idiot," an unfamiliar voice speaks up, and whoever it is, they make that silly little emotion Abigale warned about flutter in my chest.

No! I can't. I can't like how one of them sounds. I can't. I refuse.

He turns off the light, and the familiar glow of the lamp Wolf carries replaces it.

What's going on?

A hand touches my shoulder, the first touch I've had since I've been down here, and I scream, doing my best to get away. The chains tug against my body, effectively stopping me. "Please, please, don't," I cry to him, the first wet tears I've had since Abigale left. "Don't hurt me. I'll do anything!" The sobs wrench from my chest like someone reached in themselves and ripped them out. "Please," I say pathetically, scooting back as far as I can without meeting the man's eyes.

The small, gentle touch of his hand on my shoulder makes my body flood with warmth, and that scares me. Is he a good man? Am I so depraved for contact that any touch will do now?

"He's here to help," Wolf says. "It's okay. He's okay," he reassures me, but the terror in my stomach still twists and turns, carving my insides with a dull knife. Wolf comes closer, and the faint light enables me to see his face. The rest of the girls are crying, afraid this is the time our life ends, but when Wolf slides the lamp over to the other man, something in the back of my mind tells me it's all going to be okay.

Whoever this man is, he's beautiful. So beautiful, in fact, I have to wonder if I'm dreaming or dead because that's the only way someone like him exists. His hair is a bit shaggy and dirty blond, he has tattoos up and down his arms, and his hazel eyes flicker with a hint of gold. Maybe it's a trick of the light. Whatever it is, if this is death, I'm glad I get to see something so magnificent one last time.

"Are you here to take me upstairs?" I whisper, my voice wavering. My bravery and courage went out the door a while ago. I'm not afraid to admit that.

He bends down, coming closer to me, and I lean back, unsure of what he's doing. "No, sugar. I'm going to get you out of here. You and your friends. Your friend Abigale is safe; she told me to tell you that."

"Abigale is safe?" The relief coursing through me can't be contained. I cry again. "She's safe? Oh, god. It worked, Wolf? It worked?" I cry, my entire body shaking. "Thank you."

"We don't have much time to talk. My friend is waiting in a van outside for all of you. We need to get you out, okay?" He cups my face and exhales a breath that's shaken and unsteady, like he's about to break. "What's your name?"

"Scarlett," I say as Wolf hands him the key to the locks trapping me here.

"I'll get the rest of the girls free. We need to hurry. We don't have much time. My sister can come with you. I can stay with you. I'll have a bounty on my head."

"You'll be safe. I swear it," the man says. "We need to hurry." He looks around the basement and growls. "I can't believe they've done this. I won't stand for it." The man, who has yet to tell me his name, slides the key into the lock around my neck. When the metal gives, I reach up angrily and throw it as far as I can, gasping for air. "Hey, hey, Scarlett, sugar, look at me." The man cups my face again and gives me a kind smile, but something in his eyes, something a bit dark, lurks in their depths. "My name is Boomer. You're going to be just fine. Okay? I'm going to get you out of here."

I nod and hold out my hands as he unlocks the shackles too. "Okay," I utter, a bit high-pitched and whiny, but I can't help it; I can't stop the damn tears. I'm relieved. The bracelets fall free, and next are my ankles. Once I'm free, I throw myself around Boomer's neck and hold on tight. I never want to let go.

I'm safe.

He's safe.

"I got you, sugar. You aren't ever going to live in fear again. I got you." He kisses my temple and lifts me into his arms. I haven't realized how cold I am until I'm against his warm chest. I lay my head against the strong beat of his heart, and the shirt he wears soaks in the wetness on my cheek.

"You're real," I whisper against him as he carries me up the steps.

"I'm real. Your nightmare is over. You hear me?" he says. "Close your eyes. I don't want you to see this place."

I listen to him without hesitation. I don't want to see this place ever again. I have enough nightmares to last me a lifetime. When we get done climbing the staircase, I know we're in the main part of the house, or wherever I'm at. I try to snuggle against my savior, trying to bury my face into his chest. I wish I could crawl inside of it and wear his body like a shield, but I can't.

His hand cups the back of my head, and he shushes me gently. "It's alright. We're almost out of here, sugar. You never have to see this place again. It's about to get really bright, okay? Keep those pretty blue eyes shut for me."

I tighten my arms around his neck and press my face against his throat, inhaling the scent on his skin. He smells like sweat, like he's been outside all day, and a bar of soap. No cologne, no aftershave, or whatever men use, just simple musk, and I love it.

His throat moves up and down from my gesture. I guess I'm being pretty obvious here, but I don't care. He has no idea what he's done for me, for my soul, by releasing me from this hellhole. He's breathed life back into me when I thought it had been taken away forever.

And I can't help but be a little bit in love with him—a man I don't even know. I know I shouldn't feel anything toward men right now, but as I'm cradled in his arms, how can I be afraid of him when he saved me from a life of torture and abuse?

The van door opens, and an old man wearing big glasses comes to view. He looks kind, like a grandpa, and his eyes soften and water when they see me. "Oh goodness me, you poor thing," he says, staring at me with pity and sadness. I guess I can see why. I'm nearly naked, in a dirty bra and underwear I've been wearing for days now … weeks, maybe? I'm not sure.

I turn my face into Boomer's chest. He tries to put me down in the seat, but I cling to him and shake my head. "Please, don't let me go. Don't let me go," I repeat as I dig my nails into his neck until I know I break skin.

Wolf places the other girls in the van, and the old man covers them with a blanket. He has an extra one in his hand as he waits for Boomer to set me down.

Boomer reaches up and wraps the blanket around me, all while keeping me in his arms. "I'm never going to let you go, sugar. You never have to ask me twice," he says, opening the passenger-side door. He pulls out something round and green, and my eyes widen when I finally realize what it is.

It's a grenade.

"Homer, start the van because we'll have all of about five seconds to get the fuck out of here. Wolf, get settled. I'm not kidding," Boomer warns, half of his body in the van while the other half hangs out. "I need you to hold on tight, okay? I won't be able to make it back inside the vehicle before this goes off, and we're going to be moving. You're going to get scared, but I'm not going to let anything happen to you. Do you believe me?"

I shouldn't believe him. I only know his name, and his name doesn't sound real.

"I believe you," I answer stupidly, and a wicked shine takes over the chocolate abyss of his eyes.

"That's my girl," he says. Hearing him call me his girl makes me blush. He bites the clip and yanks it away from the bomb, spits it out, and throws it into the front door. "Go, go, go!" he says, his arms wrapping around me tight as Homer speeds out of the driveway. We don't get far before the ground shakes and the windows rattle. "Wooo!" Boomer howls in the air before dipping his head under the frame of the window to sit in the seat. He slams the door then reaches behind him to buckle us in.

"Shit, kid, I knew you were fucked somehow. You're just fucked in the head, ain't ya?" the old man says to Boomer.

"Shut up and drive, Homer." Boomer chuckles, and the shake of his chest makes me almost smile, but the realization of what took place hasn't sunk in yet.

"You are. You're a goddamn mental case. Do I need to worry about you blowing my motel up? You're going to have to blow me up with it."

"Homer, shut up or I will blow it up." I can hear the tease in Boomer's voice, and Homer mumbles something under his breath that I can't understand, but Boomer does, and he laughs again.

Even his laugh is warm and takes the cold away from my body.

I really hope being in his arms is a dream because waking up would be the worst nightmare.

CHAPTER SEVEN

Boomer

T HE WOMAN IN MY ARMS IS THE WOMAN I'M MEANT TO SPEND the rest of my life with. When I saw her, something clicked inside. This roaring need to keep her safe and get her out of that fucking place took over. She looked so small, chained up like a damn animal, in a dirty bra and panties. I know for certain I'm going to kill every last one of these motherfuckers when I can.

They're going to be pissed that I rescued their hostages, and they're going to want retaliation.

We come to a secluded area, thick with trees and brush. Homer's Bronco is hidden in here somewhere. We're going to ditch the van I rented under a fake name and burn the bitch. My cock hasn't been so hard in ages. While the beautiful girl in my arms has a little something to do with it, the grenade, explosion, and the fire I'm about to set? Fuck.

If I was alone, I'd jerk off and watch the flames dance in the sky, moving fluidly like a seductive lover.

Hey, I never said I wasn't fucked in the head.

"Okay, everyone. We're switching cars; come on. Hurry, hurry. We don't have much time before they blaze this city with their fury." I usher the girls out, and Wolf helps them into the Bronco. Homer hurries the best he can, and I try to put Scarlett down, but she holds onto me like a spider monkey. Don't get me wrong, I fucking love it, but I don't want her to get hurt.

Scarlett. What a hot name. I never met anyone with that name before, and I want to say it over and over and over again. I'm not sure what the future holds for us, with what she's been through, but I'll be patient, and I hope she can be patient with me because I'm all kinds of damaged and torn.

I hope, in time, she doesn't give up on me because I swear, in the end, I'm worth it. I don't know how I am. I can give a list of reasons why I'm not good enough for her, that I'm too fucked for her, especially with everything she's been through, but there's one thing I know that's worthy of something—my heart. My head might be my enemy right now, but my heart means well.

I mean well. That has to be enough, right?

"I have to set this thing on fire, sugar. I'll be right back. Wolf will take you with the other girls. You'll be alright." I call her sugar because she looks all sweet and delicious, something that can be bad but good for me all at the same time. I know once I taste her, whenever that may be, I'll be addicted.

She shakes her head again, the headful of long black hair shines blue in the light, and I run my fingers over her face, noticing a bruise on her cheek. Rage burns deep inside as I realize they hurt her. Our eyes meet, for the first time in broad daylight, and the color of her irises rob my breath. They're the color of blue fire, the hottest flame, and that's when I always know the fire is at its best.

Oh, this woman is made for me.

"You're going to be okay, Scarlett. I promise. I don't want to burn you," I say, ironic that I want to burn everything around her to keep her safe.

"You won't," she whispers. "I'm not ready for you to let me go, unless you want to."

Hell no, I don't want to.

"You're about to get a peek that maybe I'm not all there in the head, sugar."

"I figured that out when you tossed a grenade and smiled about it."

"That doesn't bother you?"

She shakes her head. "No, just don't ever chain me."

I offer her the lighter fluid in my hand, so she can have the honors. "Never. I promise." This connection between us is as quick as lighting a match, and it's obvious she feels it too. She doesn't know this, but she will in time, but the only chains between us link us together. I've felt this way since the moment I laid eyes on her.

I probably need to cool it down. She's in shock and probably has no idea what's happening right now, and she won't remember anything once the adrenaline crashes. I push that thought away because it hurts more than it should, considering I've known this chick all of two minutes. "You do the honors. You deserve it."

She takes the bottle and opens it with her mouth, making me hold back a groan when a bit of lighter fluid squirts in her mouth, and she spits it out like a fucking professional. Does the taste not bother her? One hand stays around my neck, and she squirts the fluid all over the van. I walk around slowly, letting her take her time. I can't stop watching her.

She's enjoying it.

I see the madness taking over her eyes, the anger, the revenge, and everything around me fades. The wind stops blowing, the birds stop chirping, and all I can focus on is the slight insane glee on her face. She squeezes until the bottle is empty, and then she throws it in the van. "What now?" she asks, her voice hoarse from the iron collar that was around her neck.

I take out my matchbook. "It's time to put it behind you, sugar." It's difficult, but I manage to get a match out and hand it to her, holding the black strip close so she can light it. "Go ahead."

Scarlett swipes it, igniting it in one motion, and the scratch against the red matchhead is music to my ears. She stares at the dancing flame and then tosses it. In slow motion, the match flips, and I take a few steps back to get away from the blistering heat we're about to feel.

It lands on the white frame of the van, and blue flames, like her eyes, spread out quickly, engulfing the van before orange and yellow reach for the sky.

"We need to go."

"Can we wait? I want to watch it burn," she says darkly, staring at the black smoke cascading up toward the clouds.

"I'll let you burn whatever you want later, sugar. We have to go. I need to get you ladies to safety."

She yawns, and it's followed by a groan. "I don't feel good, Boomer."

"I know you don't, sugar. I hope it's the last time you ever feel like this," I say earnestly, knowing the stress, malnourishment, shock, and adrenaline are all overwhelming her. It's only a matter of time before she crashes.

"Don't let me go," she urges, wrapping those small arms around my neck again.

I never want to let her go, but I can't tell her that. She'll run away, and I don't own her, no matter how much I want to. She has a family, people who miss her, I assume, and when she leaves, because she will, I'll miss her.

I'm already dreading the day. No one else will feel as perfect in my arms as Scarlett does. The only person who needs to worry about someone letting go is me.

Fuck, here I go. I'm being obsessive, which isn't new since I'm an obsessive person. I'm really nervous that Scarlett is going to be a compulsion. Compulsions are so dangerous, but I'd feel so much relief if I got to have her.

So much.

I walk to the passenger side of the Bronco and slide in. Homer reverses, the tires crunching over the leaves, and as we drive past the van, the heat from the blaze hits my face, and I relish in it. The air immediately gets cooler the further we drive away from it. I look down to see Scarlett has fallen asleep against my chest. I push her hair out of the way with my finger, like I did earlier, and I take in all her features, memorizing them, searing them into my mind. I never want to forget.

When I'm old and out of my mind, more than I already am, and the only thing I can remember is my youth, I want to remember Scarlett like this. I want to remember her trusting me when I'm sure she didn't want to. I want to remember the glowing wildfire of her irises when I first locked my gaze with hers. I want to remember the soft curves of her jaw, the length of her lashes, the blue hue of her hair…

Damn it, I want to remember everything about her.

"You're out of your mind," Homer says, taking his eyes off the road for a split second to look at me.

"Don't I know it," I whisper, not wanting to wake Scarlett up by speaking too loudly. Her ear is right against my chest, and I know the vibrations can interrupt her sound sleep.

"No, really. She's out of your league, and she has a lot of healing to do."

"Wow, Homer. Thanks," I snort.

"She is," Wolf chimes in. "Has the heart of a lion too. She ripped me a new one for not doing enough, but I did try. I did." He looks over at the girls asleep on either side of him. "I should have done more. She was right. She's the only reason Abigale got to you."

"Abigale's not in the best shape. She's really ill, and that gunshot wound isn't helping." I want to know what happened, but rolling down memory lane isn't the best thing to do right now. Emotions are running high, but the only person who matters to me is Scarlett.

"That's my fault," Wolf speaks up. "Scarlett came up with the idea, and Abigale agreed because she was so sick, but it had to look like I took care of the problem, you know? I had to make it believable until help arrived … *if* help arrived."

"I understand," I say. He has no idea how much I relate.

"I had to," he explains himself. "My sister—"

"Hey," I cut him off. He feels like he has to explain himself, but he doesn't owe me any answers. Not right now, at least. "Don't. I get it, okay? No one blames you. I know you blame yourself, but that's something you have to figure out on your own. You have to come to terms with it. You did what you thought was right for you and yours and, man, that's all you can do. It's behind you now, and whatever lies ahead is going to be rough, so you need to be ready. There is no room for self-pity or blame. This is war; you get me. Fucking war. I need your head in the game. Everyone's head. We have to win because this can't happen again." I point with my eyes to the girls on either side of him and tighten my hold around Scarlett. "This is cruel."

"Yes, sir," he says, and the proclamation makes me feel sick.

"Don't call me that. It's Boomer, or you can call me Jenkins, but not sir."

"I'm just thinking, maybe if they had a leader like you, none of this would have happened," Wolf says.

I stare down at Scarlett, brushing her soft hair back. While I wish I could've been there to stop this shit from happening, I'm no leader. I'm a fucking wreck. I'm what they call a temporary fix. That's all I am, and that's all I'll ever be. "No, man. I'm the last thing anyone needs," I say it more to Scarlett than to Wolf. She can do better than me. She doesn't deserve someone who battles their mind every day. She's dealt with enough.

Selfishly, I want her to deal with me. I want her to fix me because I have no idea how to fix myself. The booze, the women, I've even done drugs—none of it makes it go away, but Scarlett and those fire blue eyes lessen my pain, my self-torment.

What do I need to blow up or burn down to figure out how I can get her to never let go of me? Because I need someone to hold on to.

CHAPTER EIGHT

Scarlett

I WAKE UP TO THE SMELL OF COFFEE. IT DRIPS INTO THE POT, steaming to alert that it's almost done. My back is against something soft, and I moan when I feel the pillow under my head. I'll never take for granted something as common as a bed again, not when my bones still hurt from the cement ground I sat on for too long.

I try to sit up, but my skin rubs against the cover, and I whimper. It's raw and scratched, just like an open wound. My eyes flutter open, ready to see a dark room with wet walls and no light, but I don't. The sun peeks through the window, and a breeze comes through the screen. I inhale, smelling the salt and the sea. I can hear the waves lightly crashing against the shore, and my emotions spike. I want to cry, but only happy tears.

I'm really out of that basement. I never thought I'd see

the ocean again, hear it, or feel the sun. I concluded that my life was doomed.

"Hey." The familiar voice of my hero makes me turn over to see him sitting at the small round table in a chair that looks like it can barely hold his weight. He's a big guy, tall, and really handsome. I can't help but stare at him and all his hard angles. "You're up. I was getting worried. You slept for so long."

"What do you mean? It's only morning." I yawn and try to stretch, but my body hurts too damn much.

He stands, and that's when I notice he isn't wearing a shirt. I glance away, not wanting to get caught staring at him. He has tattoos, so many tattoos, just like the biker guys who kidnapped me, but I know he's better than them. He's proven otherwise. Heat rises in my cheeks, and I close my eyes, wishing the damn blush away. I hate my pale skin. It always tells what I'm feeling, and I can't stand it.

Boomer's wide-set shoulders and firm pecs make me feel something I shouldn't want to feel—desire.

"Scarlett, it's nearly sunset. You've been here two days, sugar. You were exhausted. I can't say I blame you." His voice becomes soft, lightening the masculine depth it usually holds.

"Oh, wow. That long? I still feel like I could sleep for days." My voice sounds like I've swallowed a ten-pound bag of rocks. I reach my hand up to touch my neck and feel the raised, chapped skin where the collar was.

I'm not there anymore. I'm not there anymore. They can't hurt me.

"Go right ahead. I've been keeping watch, so has Wolf and Homer. You're safe here. I promise." The way he looks at me as he says those words, it's almost as if he's saying he'll slay dragons if it means keeping me safe.

Damn him and his intense gaze.

He grabs a shirt from the other chair and slips it on to cover his beautiful body. *No! He's the best thing I've seen since that piece of bread I ate a few days ago. Take it off! Take the damn shirt off!*

"Sorry about the room. I know it isn't the nicest. I'm working with Homer to repair this place and get it in tip-top shape." The shirt falls to his hips, hiding the flawless skin. Part of the shirt on the left side is caught somehow, rolled up to show skin.

I manage to push myself up and lean against the headboard, never taking my eyes off the small patch of flesh. My eyes follow him as he strides over to the coffee pot on the dresser. Even his walk is smooth yet determined, powerful and graceful all at the same time. "The room is amazing. It's much better than the alternative," I say, gathering the sheets to cover my body. I'm in a big black T-shirt, but I still feel vulnerable and naked. I'm still in my dirty underwear and bra, and as much as I want to change, I'm happy that Boomer respected me enough to keep them on. The thought of any man seeing me naked right now, after knowing what was about to happen to me... I'm relieved to know the only thing Boomer did was cover me.

"Shit, you're right. I'm sorry. I should have thought. I'm fucking stupid. I'm sorry." He slaps his head with his palm, telling himself over and over again how worthless he is. It isn't a new thing, that much I know. This looks like a habit.

"Hey, you aren't stupid, and you aren't worthless. You saved my life; does that sound like someone who is stupid or worthless? I'd be someone's whore if it wasn't for you." I take a deep breath from the harsh words, but they're true. I can't look around. I can't bury it, or pretty it up and put a bow on it. That was going to be my life.

He stares at me while holding the side of his head, scratching his scalp. There's torment in his eyes, a secret I don't know, but he's battling himself. "It's not just that," I think he said, but he spoke so low, I could hardly hear. "Anyway." He clears his throat. "Do you want coffee? I've been making a fresh pot every few hours just in case you woke up. I have some pain medicine too. It's just Tylenol, but until I find a doctor, it's the best I can do."

"Coffee would be great. Thank you," I reply, watching his every move. I never take my eyes off him because I find him fascinating. He pours two cups and puts the pot back in its place before turning around and coming my way. Boomer hands me a simple white mug, something similar to what a diner would have, and that's when I notice he's missing a finger. I don't keep my eyes on it too long because I'm not sure I want to know yet, and I don't want to make him uncomfortable, but I am curious.

The jagged scar tells me whatever happened was painful, and that hurts my heart for him.

"Sorry, I don't have creamer or sugar, *sugar*." He chuckles, winking at me with those long, thick lashes framing his chocolate eyes, and I look away and stare at the steam rising from my coffee instead. "Plus, I like it black. All that shit in it doesn't really make it coffee, does it?" he asks, slurping the hot java down.

"No, I suppose not. I drink it black too, so no need for all that shit," I say, and when he hears the curse word fall from my lips he laughs.

"Never thought someone as pretty as you would say such a thing."

He thinks I'm pretty. My heart is beating at a fatal rate, and I'm not able to form words to reply. I just drink my coffee because I don't know what else to do.

"Shit, I'm sorry. I shouldn't have said that. I'm sure you aren't wanting to hear shit like that right now."

"It's okay," I say, not wanting to admit no one has ever given me such a sweet compliment before. My eyes drift to his hand again, to the finger that isn't there, as I drink my coffee. We fall into a comfortable silence. I don't feel the need to say anything; just having him near me is peaceful. I groan when I readjust my sitting position, and the mug falls out of my hands because the quick stab of pain on my right butt cheek takes me by surprise. "Oh my god, I'm so sorry. My skin hurts so much!" My eyes start to well, and Boomer bends over to grab the mug off the floor.

"It's alright. Really, it's fine. It can be cleaned up."

"My skin hurts so bad," I whimper, the pain too much to bear. I'm not sure why it's suddenly hitting me so hard, but I can't stand it. I feel like my flesh is falling off.

He cups my face gently, not rubbing my red cheeks, so he doesn't hurt me, and he nods, like he understands the pain I'm going through. "I know, sugar. I know it does. Your skin is in pretty bad shape being down there on the wet concrete like that. I've put some salve on it, and that numbed it up, but it must be wearing off. I got you some stuff to take a soothing oatmeal bath too. I wish I could take your pain away; I really do." He pushes the tangled mess of my hair behind my shoulder, and I look at my hands, wrinkled, peeling, chapped and pink. My fingers look like prunes, but I haven't soaked in a bath for too long.

I guess I have. I sat in a puddle of water and my own piss

for days. It makes sense that I'm so disgusting right now. I don't even know how Boomer can stand to be near me. I'm sure I'm a nightmare to look at. "I'm sorry this has landed in your lap, Boomer. Once I'm healed—"

"It isn't a hardship, sugar. It really isn't."

If I'm not mistaken, his eyes fall to my lips, but it's so quick I'm wondering if I'm imagining things. I want him to kiss me, I realize. I want to feel his big lips against mine. I've never seen a man with lips like his before. They're perfect. His bottom lip is the same size as the top, thick and plush; the kind a woman can get lost in for hours and hours to forget time.

Then suddenly she is naked with him on top of her.

Yeah, those kinds of lips.

I look away from him, needing to take a breath. "How are my friends?" I ask. I should have asked earlier, but Boomer has a way of making me forget, and I need that right now because I want to forget everything.

His hands fall from my face, and his palm rubs over the stubble along his jawline. "They're alright. I can't remember her name, but one of them is very sick, but she isn't as bad as Abigale. Abigale needs a doctor; she's getting worse every day. I'm pretty sure that gunshot wound is infected. You can see them later, if you want," he offers. "I'll take you to them."

"I don't think I can move right now," I admit. "Can I have that Tylenol?"

"Yeah, sugar. You can have whatever you want." He stands up, placing both coffee mugs on the round table, and he walks over to the dresser and grabs the bottle of Tylenol. He opens it effortlessly and pours four into his hand. He grabs a bottle of water from the mini fridge, opens it, and then he hands them over to me.

"Thank you, Boomer."

"Whatever you need, I'm here."

I roll the white tabs in my palm and toss them into my mouth, following it with a cold gulp of water. *Oh, that tastes good.* I keep drinking it, wanting more—needing more. The water flows out of the corner of my mouth as I chug it.

"Woah, hey. Stop, slow down, sugar. Slow. You're going to make yourself sick." Boomer gently wraps his hand around the bottle and pulls it from my lips. I'm breathing hard, and I try to reach for it again, but he holds it away from me. "I know. You're dehydrated, but you have to take things slow. Your body isn't used to this, okay? I'm going to put the rest in the fridge. I want to make sure you don't throw it up."

He means well, but I want the water so bad. "Please, Boomer. I'm so thirsty." It's amazing that I had no idea until the water hit my tongue.

"I know, sugar." He runs his index finger along my jawline. "I'm just looking out for you. How about I draw you a nice bath, and you can get cleaned up? I got you new clothes and under ... things." His cheeks turn a bright shade of red when he mentions bra and panties. He's had to have taken off a lot of them, so why is he so coy about it? "I uh..." He coughs into his fist. "I looked at your bra size to find out. You were sleeping. I'm sorry. I just wanted to get clean clothes for you."

The aggravation I felt about the water quickly disappears. He must have felt so out of his comfort zone when he got my clothes. He's so sweet. "You didn't have to do that, but thank you. I can't wait to feel clean."

"Not going to let you stay in dirty clothes, just like the others. Your life is yours now. It doesn't belong to anyone."

Just like the others. I'm not special to him. I need to

remember that. Boomer is being kind, and I'm falling head over heels in love with a man who's just doing the right thing.

"How about I fix you a bath?" he asks.

I nod, tucking my hair behind my ear. "That would be great."

"And maybe after, you can call your parents? Or husband, boyfriend…" He leaves the sentence open, the muscle in his jaw flexing.

I hold back a whimper when I move my legs to the edge of the bed, swinging them over to get myself to the restroom. "No husband or boyfriend. I do have parents, but I don't want to call. Not yet." It's probably the wrong decision, but I know they'll want to come wherever I am, and with how I look and feel, I don't want to burden them with that. My feelings are enough to deal with. I can't handle theirs right now. It's selfish, but I need time.

"Whatever you want, sugar. I'd like to hear about them."

I push myself up, and my knees give out. I fall back to land on the bed; even with the soft top, I know it's going to hurt.

But Boomer is there. He catches me, one arm around my waist, and the other swoops down and lifts me up off the floor. "I'm here, okay? Let me help you."

What happens when he isn't here? What happens when I'm alone? I don't ever want to be alone again, especially in the dark.

CHAPTER NINE

Boomer

T HIS WOMAN IS GOING TO TEST ME. I CAN ALREADY SEE BITS OF her personality coming out. She's independent and likes to do things on her own, and that's too fucking bad. I'm going to be here. I'm going to take care of her, and she's going to see that she never has to be alone again.

The words from earlier whisper in my mind, reminding me that I don't deserve her.

Stupid. Worthless. Crazy. Go kill them. Go kill them. Go kill them.

It won't stop. It's a record on repeat and breaking it's the most difficult thing I've ever had to overcome. I don't know how to make it stop.

"Hey, are you okay?" Scarlett asks, touching my chin with her fragile fingertips. I want to bend down and kiss them, shower them with love, but I don't know how. I don't love myself, so how do I go about showing it to someone else when on a good day, I hate myself at best?

"What? I'm fine, sugar. I promise." I place her on the olive-green toilet seat as gently as I can. I know how much her skin hurts, and the last thing I want to do is hurt her. I lean down and turn the hot and cold handles at the same time. They're those old flower looking handles that beach homes have from the damn nineties. I can't wait to make this place my own. First thing I'm changing is the bathroom. It's cringe worthy.

I place the stopper at the bottom and pour some lavender soothing oil I found at the store in the tub. It smells good. I thought women liked bath shit, so why not stock up on it. Then I scoop some oatmeal jasmine mix in there and stir it up. "I want you to place your hand in there to make sure it doesn't sting, okay? Come here." I hold out my arm for her, and she squats next to me. I roll the sleeve up on her shirt and grin. My clothes are so big on her, and she looks so sexy; even my cock has taken notice, but I've hidden it.

It's been so long since I've reacted to a woman that I forgot what it's like. All the women got old; I've just been looking for the one I want at my side. I place her hand in the water, covering it with mine, and she sighs in content. "That feels good," she says. "It's soothing."

I'm relieved. "Good. I'm glad. I'll leave you alone—"

"No!" her hand flies out of the water, gripping my arm and soaking my shirt. She sees where she's holding me and lets go. "Please, don't go. I don't want to be alone."

"It's okay, sugar. I'll be here. You want me to close the curtain?"

"No," she hurries out. "I don't want to feel trapped. I ... I might need your help washing my hair too."

Of course, she'll need help.

Stupid. Stupid. Stupid. Worthless. Just end it already. Stop being a burden to the world. Nothing you do is right. Kill yourself. Kill yourself. Kill yourself.

"You're doing it again," she whispers. "You're in your head."

"I'm fine," I say, not wanting to get into my demons. "Let's get you in this bath, sugar. Lift your arms." She does as I ask, and the tips of my fingers skim over her ribs. Scarlett inhales, and her cheeks turn that pretty shade of red. I swallow, not wanting to show that her body is affecting me. She's a beautiful woman, half-naked right now; of course, I'm going to react, but I'm not going to do anything about it. Now isn't the time or place for that, especially when she doesn't need someone like me.

When I see the state of her body, my lust dies down and the urge to kill, the need, it takes over. The words 'kill them, kill them, kill them' repeat in my head. Her ribs show from the lack of food, she has skin sores everywhere, and harsh scratches from the cement. Her bra used to be white, but now it's this ugly brown color mixed with speckles of red, which I'm assuming is blood. I take a deep, shaky breath to calm myself before the rage takes over and I go blowing things up that don't need to be.

I toss the shirt over my shoulder and she turns around, giving me the long canvas of her back. Fuck, she's pretty. A bit thin from being captive, but I'll make everything better; I'll make her better, and she'll never suffer again.

Not being able to control myself, I run my finger from the back of her nape down the middle of her spine until I come to the strap of her bra. I flick it off effortlessly, like I've done a dozen other times. The material falls to either side of her, and she uncrosses her arms, the straps on her shoulders loosening. I slip my finger under it and slide it down her arm, careful not to rub the material against the open wound beside the strap.

I do the same to the other side, and then the bra falls to her feet. I close my eyes as I slide her underwear down her legs, wanting to look at her ass but not wanting to look while she's so vulnerable and not feeling like herself. If she wants my eyes on her, I want her to tell me.

Her underwear are off and on the floor, and I turn around immediately, staring at the ugly floral wallpaper that makes up the room next to us.

"Just let me know when you need me," I say, placing my hands over my growing erection. Out of all the damn times, why do I get one now? "Go away," I hiss at it.

"Did you say something?" she asks, and the splash of water tells me she's climbed in the bathtub.

I let out a breath I didn't realize I was holding. "No, sorry. Nothing. Do your thing," I say, thinking about the time I got my finger cut off, the agony, the blood, the gunshot, and that makes the erection wilt in record time.

I'm glad I'm not broken. So many times I tried to fuck a cut-slut, but I couldn't get it up. I was done with them, done sharing, done with the mindless drunk fucks, and I wasn't attracted to them anymore.

A woman like Scarlett, though? I'd have to be a dead man not to react to such beauty.

Scarlett whimpers behind me, and I push my hands on the floor and slide until my back hits the tub. "What is it? Are you okay?"

"It hurts. I can't reach some spots because my skin stretches. I'm fine."

"Cover up, and I'll help you if you want. I know it will take trust, but I swear on my life, I won't touch you that way." At least, not right now; not until she's healed physically and mentally.

There's no hope for me to be healed. I'll forever be fucked in the head.

"I trust you, Boomer." The water ripples again, telling me she's getting into place. "I'm ready."

I turn around and give her a wide smile. "Hi," I say lamely.

"Hi." She lays her cheek on her knee, hiding half her lips, but I can tell she's smiling. Scarlett hands me the washcloth, our fingers brushing when I grab it, and my world tilts, just like every other time we touch.

Her breasts are hidden by her thighs, the fatty flesh plumping from the pressure. The position should look erotic, but the way she holds her knees to her chest makes her look small and vulnerable. I rub the cloth over her neck, careful not to irritate the skin more than it already is. I fucking hate those bikers. Her neck is bruised from that damn collar. The wound itself is three inches wide and wraps all the way around.

"I'm sorry if it hurts," I say, squeezing water from the cloth so it falls down her shoulders.

"It's okay. I'm used to it."

"You shouldn't be." I move to her back and just dip the rag into the water and clench it in my fist, so the water is kind to what hurts. I don't want to rub anything. It will hurt too much.

I bathe her like that, and I find that I want to do this every night. I want to take care of her, wash her clean of the day, of her pain, and make her feel safe. I dip the cloth in the water again and bring it to her face. The skin isn't as bad as other places, but I'm still gentle, wiping away the dirt to reveal white, flawless skin. "Wow," I say in awe. I don't mean for the compliment to leave my lips, but I can't stop it. Her wet lashes fan, a few sections of the long hair clump together, and it makes her eyes look brighter, bigger, and I'm lost.

I'm a fucking goner.

"What?" she asks innocently. "I know. I look terrible." Scarlett looks away from me while grabbing her hair.

I move the cloth under her chin and turn her head, making her look at me. Doesn't she know that even on her worst day, she's the most beautiful thing I've ever laid eyes on? "I was just thinking how pretty your eyes are."

She bites her bottom lip but doesn't say anything. It's fine. I don't need her to. I can tell she likes the compliment, but she doesn't know what to say. "I have shampoo and conditioner if you want to wash your hair."

"I do. If you can save it," she mumbles. "It's a tangled wreck."

"I'll turn around so you can dip your head under the water, okay? Or maybe you want to try to shower instead? The bath water is looking a bit murky."

She glances down, and the look on her face is pure horror. Fuck, I've embarrassed her. That voice that says I'm stupid tries to take over, but somehow, I push it back and take care of the woman in front of me, not worrying about myself. "This is nothing. When I'm out of the shop every day, back home, I have to take two showers just to get the grease off my body. Really."

"You must think I'm disgusting," she says.

"I think you're a person who went through something traumatic. You could never be disgusting." My voice comes out a bit harsher, and she flinches. "I'm sorry. That's just how strong I feel about the subject."

She gives me a small smile, and victory courses through me. I'm a fucking champion for putting a smile on her face, or that's what it feels like. "I'll shower," she answers, and pride swells in my chest for her. She wants to try it on her own, and it won't be easy.

"I'll be right here if you need me." I feel like I've said it a million times, but I want her to always know that loneliness is something she will never have to feel again. She can always count on me.

Scarlett's fingers grip the shower curtain, and she shuts her eyes, taking a deep breath. I don't say anything. I let her decide. She's obviously fighting the urge to close the curtain, but she does. Scarlett doesn't inch it shut; she jerks it all the way to the wall, covering herself.

"Good job, sugar." It might seem small to some, but her closing that curtain is a big deal. While she isn't alone in the room, she's alone in an enclosed space. She's fighting a fear, and she isn't letting it control her.

I need to take note.

I let my own vices control me, every day.

"Boomer?"

The way she says my name, soft and quiet, like a breeze carrying a distant howl, makes me relax. I sit on the toilet lid and lean back. "Sugar?"

"Is that your real name?"

"No," I say quickly. "My ... stepdad called me Boomer because I have a thing with fire, if you haven't noticed. My name is Jenkins."

"Jenkins," she giggles. "I like Boomer more, actually. It suits you."

I lean forward and tap my boots on the floor. "So I've

heard," I say, chuckling when I remember how I got the name in the first place.

"Where are you from?"

Shit. She's going to start asking questions I sure as hell do not want to answer. If she ever finds out I'm from another Ruthless King chapter, she'll leave. I'll have no chance with her, and I can't risk that. "Um, Vegas, actually. Had some family drama and needed to get away," I tell her, bypassing the truth a bit, but not exactly telling her a lie either.

"I understand." Scarlett is so much more talkative when she hides herself. I'm going to have to make sure she feels comfortable enough without a barrier between us, like this shower curtain. "My parents and I got into a fight before I got taken. They're controlling, but they love me; they mean well."

"Are you sure you don't want to call them, sugar? I know they would be happy to hear from you." I fucking wish I could call my dad. I miss him like crazy. Every damn day.

"I don't want them to see me like this."

I hate it when she sounds sad. I know they miss her because the thought of her being gone has me missing her.

She hisses, "Ow. Oh, damn it."

"What? What is it? Are you okay?" I'm up and off the toilet in a flash, and I'm about to yank the shower curtain open when she answers.

"I have soap in my eye."

I hang my head and take my hand off the curtain. I'm glad she isn't in pain in some way. The shower shuts off, and I take a step back, ramming my head against the edge of the door, and I groan as the curtain opens.

"Are you okay?" She yelps, slipping in the slick tub. She grabs onto the shower curtain, but I dive for her, so she doesn't hurt herself. The curtain rips from the rod, and she falls onto me. The weight of her is unexpected, and it makes me tip over.

Oh, this is not going to be good.

I wrap my arms around her as tight as I can and maneuver us to make sure I take the force of the fall. My back slams against the floor, the air knocking from my lungs. Water from her body soaks my clothes, and when I look at her to make sure she is okay, her small tits are pressed against my chest, and a droplet of water slides between the valley.

Fuck.

She's naked.

And every inch of her body is molding against me perfectly. Hip to hips, chest to chest, nearly lips to lips.

Scarlett is made for me.

End of fucking story.

CHAPTER TEN

Scarlett

I HAVE NO WORDS FOR WHAT JUST HAPPENED.

There was a dollop of conditioner on the tub floor, and my foot slipped against it. It was like slow motion falling toward Boomer. I couldn't stop it, and then he caught me, holding me to his chest so I wouldn't get hurt.

There is no way there's another man as good as him.

And now, my hands are against his chest, soaking the white t-shirt to his skin. His nipples peek through, and my mouth waters when I see they're pierced. Simple bars, not hoops, and I want nothing more than to pull them into my mouth and play.

He feels so defined and hard. His abs clench under me, and that's when I realize I'm on top of him, nude, and the shower curtain is covering us like a blanket. My wet hair falls around us like a veil, our faces inches apart, and his breath tickles my lips causing them to tingle.

"Sugar, I want nothing more than to kiss you right now," he tells me while staring at my lips before sliding his eyes up to mine. His hand parts my hair, lightly caressing my jaw. My nerves flutter, a million butterflies flapping their wings in my stomach. I lick my lips, hoping he kisses me. "But you aren't ready for that, and as much as I want to, fuck, I really want to kiss you, Scarlett. More than anything in this world, but not before you're ready."

"I—Boomer," I stutter. I can't say the words. I can't form them.

He's right. I'm not ready, and no matter how much I want to be, it doesn't change the fact that I'm not ready to feel his lips, when only a few days ago I was meant to do so much more than that to other men. I have to get over that first.

"It's okay," he reassures. "I'll be here when you are. I'm not going anywhere." He brings my head down and places a kiss on my forehead. His unwavering support sinks into me, mending a piece of my broken soul together. It's a small piece, but something is better than nothing, and it tells me I'm on my way to where I need to be.

And that place is with Boomer, my lips against his.

"Come on; let's get you up." He rolls us, and in one strong move, I'm in his arms again.

He never looks down at my exposed breasts. Boomer stares ahead, but I can tell he wants nothing more than to look. He fights the urge as he sits me down and grabs a towel, closing his eyes as he wraps the soft cotton around me. His shoulders sag when my body is covered.

I want his arms around me, anchoring me to this reality, the here, the now. It's so easy to think about the past, what was, what could have been. Boomer changed my path. Wherever life leads me, I hope it's kind enough to lead me right next to Boomer. Living without him, without my life vest, I'll drown. He keeps me afloat. I don't know him well, not at all actually, but I think I'm meant to know him. I'm meant to be here.

"Are you okay?" he asks. His ass sways as he walks to the dresser and gets out a few pieces of clothing for me. His ass is plump, round, bigger than I thought it would be since he's in shape. He has a bubble butt. "That was a hard fall, and I know your skin is sensitive right now."

The question yanks me from my thoughts of his rear end, and blood rushes to my cheeks, no doubt turning them crimson.

He has a sideways smirk, one that's cocky and full of himself, and I love it because I know he isn't actually full of himself. Not with the constant tug of war I've seen from him. I want to know Boomer, the real him. I want to dive deeper into his mind and soul and see all the bits of good and bad that make him, him.

I bet some parts are ugly, but then the beautiful parts, the ones that outshine the bad, are going to blind me, they are so bright.

"I'm fine. That bath really helped. Maybe I just needed to get the grime off."

"Well, just in case, I think we should put this salve on your wounds. Then you're going to eat soup, and then go to bed."

"Bed? I just slept for days. I want out of the house. I want to feel the sun against my skin." Although when I look out the window, it's dark, so there goes that plan. My stomach does growl, and Boomer lets out a humorous laugh.

He lifts a brow and grabs his wallet. "I guess that tells me you want some food, huh?"

I nod and cross my arms over my stomach when a loud

grumble happens again. "I'm sorry. I feel like I haven't eaten anything in days."

His eyes soften, but there's a flick of anger, a flame of crazy that tells me he wants to do something that goes against everything I see him as. Just what makes him tick? "Sugar, you probably haven't eaten in days, at least, nothing good. I'm not really comfortable leaving you alone, so we can order in. What do you say?"

"That sounds great. After, can we maybe walk on the beach?" I whisper. "I've never been to the beach before." I'm from a small town in West Virginia. My parents worked all the time, and while they provided me with a good life, we weren't able to go on vacations. I've actually never been anywhere before.

I only remember being on campus at night when a roar of bikes pierced the night and then a pin prick in my neck. Everything after that is dark.

"You've never seen the beach?" he asks with wide, shocked eyes.

I shake my head and sit on the bed, keeping the towel wrapped around me. "No, never had the chance."

"Well, sugar, I'll make sure you get to do whatever you want in life; that I can promise." He slams the dresser drawers a little hard, and his hand comes up and grabs the sides of his head. He's muttering something, I can't figure out what, but whatever it is, it's tormenting him.

I want to help, but I don't know how.

"Boomer?"

"Yeah, sugar?"

"Are you okay?" I ask, watching him pop his neck from side to side.

"Yeah, I'm alright." He flicks his lighter on in his hand, then off, on, and off, and he stares at it for a little while before his shoulders relax. He flicks his gaze to me, and the flicker of the small flame makes the gold rings around his pupils glow.

He's beautiful. A dark, threatening beast that invokes fear, but I'm not afraid, not of Boomer. His beast, whatever the vice is, is my protector. I'll calm him when it roars its head inside him, pulling at Boomer to bring him into the shadows.

Boomer stares at me, the man that makes him gone replaced by something else; something sinister. His pupils go from wide to small dots as he focuses on me, just like a savage animal would. I don't break eye contact, and he gets confused. Just like that, the dangerous energy, the lurking demons behind his eyes disappear, and his good wins the fight.

I have an inkling that Boomer never loses a fight.

He shuts the lighter and tosses it on the table. Right as I'm about to ask him again if he's okay, his phone rings. He screens the call, then he presses ignore and shoves it in his pocket. A trickle of curiosity makes me wonder who he's ignoring. I think maybe it's another woman, and jealousy rears its nasty head, and I'm shocked. I've never had that kind of reaction to someone before.

Boomer takes a deep breath and then grabs the pile of clothes he previously pulled out for me previously and hands them to me. "Here, sugar. Why don't you get dressed, and I'll order us some food? Maybe egg drop soup for you? I'll be right outside."

"No!" I've said that word too many times. "I want you here." My voice is small, and I take the clothes from his hand and notice how soft the material is; better than anything I've ever felt. Boomer squats in front of me, and a tease of his tattoos peek from the collar of his shirt, and his hands land on my bare knees.

My pussy tingles, heat blooming across my sheath like the sun beaming across the ocean. I rub my thighs together, and Boomer's nostrils flare as if he can smell my desire. That wicked darkness inside of him comes forward, his eyes glowing again, and all I want to do is poke the bear and see how well he ravages.

I want to, but that doesn't mean I can. I don't have the bravery, not yet, but I will because I want Boomer as mine. His shirt is still wet, and I can see the large, colorful tattoo across his chest through the thin material.

And his nipples … don't get me started on his nipples.

"The way you're looking at me…" he starts, taking a few deep breaths as he shuts his eyes. "You can't look at me like that."

"Like what?"

"Like you *actually* want *me*," he says, but it's the way he says it that crushes me. He sounds as if he can't believe that I would want him. A woman who was supposed to be used up by men, and yet, he thinks I'm too good for him? I can never be good enough; that's what I truly feel and believe.

I know I'm not perfect right now, not by any means. I've lost weight, I have bruises, and my skin is pink, scratched to hell, and not pretty. I swallow the nervousness in my throat, lodged there like a damn log to suffocate me, and with a shaky hand, I reach for the towel tucked on the side near my breast. I want to undo it. I want to show him that I want him and that he can have me.

But he stops me, and my feelings are crushed. I hold the towel to my frame, embarrassed, mortified, and ashamed.

I can't believe it. Am I so desperate to feel loved? To feel wanted. Why? It was the last thing I wanted with those biker men. The very last thing, but I want Boomer to want me, regardless of how he found me. I want to feel worthy.

I want to be worthy of him.

"Hey, sugar, none of that." His wide thumb brushes under my eye, wiping a tear away.

"I'm sorry. I just… I don't know what I was thinking." I try to get up and run to the bathroom to lock myself away, but he grabs my shoulders, a soft yet firm hold on me. "Please, let me go." I beg just like I begged in the basement where the bikers lived. I hardly recognize my voice. My heart is breaking, and it's in this moment I realize how sensitive I actually am. I never knew, but the rejection from Boomer is like pouring salt on an open wound. It stings, and it's unbearable torture. How the hell am I supposed to stay here knowing I want him, and he doesn't want me?

"Look at me." His voice turns to a bite with slight authority.

I can't help but to listen.

"I am never going to let you go, you hear me?" His eyes are a raging blaze threatening to explode. "You're going to be mine, Scarlett. Not today, but one day."

"But you said—"

"No, you don't get to put words in my mouth." He lets out a shaky, distorted moan as his eyes land on where the towel is tucked in. "Sugar, you have no idea how much I want you. You're beautiful, too beautiful for the likes of me, but I'm a selfish man, and I want you for myself. I can't have you right now. You aren't ready; you're scared. When I have you"— he runs his fingers over the ridge of my collarbone, and I shiver—"When I have you, the last thing I want to see in your eyes is fear. If I didn't care about you, I'd let you take off that towel and give yourself to me, but because I do care, I can't let you do that. Not right now, sugar."

"But you want me?" I ask him, needing to hear his words of reassurance again.

"The only thing maybe you need to be afraid about is how much I want you. Once you're mine, once I have you, no one else can, sugar. There will be no one else for you, for me. It doesn't scare me. Maybe you need to be sure you want a man like me."

"What kind of man are you?"

"The kind your mother warns you about, the kind your father doesn't want you near, but the one your body can't deny." He stands and brushes the hair off my shoulder, humming in appreciation. "Now get dressed. I'm going to feed you, and then you're going to sleep. I'm not comfortable walking the beach. It's too soon for you to be out in the open."

His blunt, overly possessive words should make me feel uneasy, but it doesn't. I only have one thing on my mind now. I gulp, staring at the sleep shirt in my hand that is my size. "Can I wear your shirt to bed again?"

"You don't like what I got you? I'm sorry—"

"No, no, it isn't that." My throat turns dry, and my tongue struggles to form the words I want to say. It's a bit embarrassing. "I like your clothes. They smell like you, and I feel safe in them."

Before I can blink, I have his shirt in my hand. He has a big goofy smile on his face, one I've never seen. "Sugar, you look better in my clothes than I do. You can wear whatever you want of mine."

I give him a shy smile and look over my shoulder to see him watching me. He is so intense. I get to the bathroom and shut the door, needing a breath because Boomer steals it.

Dropping the towel, I shove his green shirt over my head and grab the front of it, and bring it to my nose to inhale. He smells so good. Wild and smoky, not from cigarettes, but a bonfire. I relax and slip on simple cotton panties. They feel so much better than the dirty ones. I don't worry with a bra. Bras suck.

The door creaks as I open it again, and Boomer is just getting off the phone. I crawl into bed and sit up, covering my legs with the blanket.

"Boomer?"

"Sugar?"

"Will … will you hold me tonight while I sleep? I had nightmares—"

"You never have to explain why you want me to hold you. I'll do it because there isn't anything more in the world I want."

I've never felt something so intense before, not so fast. Maybe it's a hero complex, maybe I see him as my savior … I don't know. What I do know is my heart has never wanted to be accepted by someone so much before.

I want to love him.

And I want his love.

It should scare me, but it doesn't; it only makes me anticipate the day I can call him mine.

CHAPTER ELEVEN

Boomer

I WAS RIGHT WHEN WE WERE IN THE BATHROOM, AND HER BODY was against mine. She fits against me perfectly. Her palm-sized tits are against me, and her leg is wrapped around my hip. The space between her legs is teasing my hard cock. It seems my body has no problem reacting to her. I feel like I'm about to explode. I haven't felt true pleasure in so long, and I want Scarlett to be the one to give it to me.

I know the wait will be worth it. I'm not going to lie; I'm fucking relieved I can get it up for a woman because for a minute, I was afraid it was just going to be me and my hand for the rest of my damn life.

I bury my nose in her hair, and she lets out a soft, sleepy moan that has my heart tripping all over itself. She nestles her face into my neck, pressing her lips against my pulse, and I wonder if she can feel my heart rate spiking in her dreams. She has to because with the way it is thudding fast and hard, I just might have a heart attack.

I inhale the lingering scent of shampoo and lazily play with her hair. She's wrapped around me like a sloth on a tree, and she presses herself harder against me anytime I move. I've never felt so wanted in my fucking life. This woman makes me feel like a king. But I need to get up. It's around eleven at night, and I know Wolf is awake still, and I need to go talk to him to see if he has found a doctor.

If only Doc were here, but I can't call because they will just bring me back home. I don't belong there anymore. I belong here. I'm not sure what my purpose is, but the fucked-up part of me has to be good for something here, and it has to deal with the Ruthless Kings Chapter in this city. I couldn't do anything about my mental turmoil at home because I knew the guys would see me as weak. I already fight that within myself, but this, this situation with the girls and this club, it's a chance to put my insanity to good use.

Not that I think I'm insane; I really don't know. I need to see a doctor again because it's scaring the shit out of me. The constant, fucked-up thoughts and statements are wearing me down. And it sounds crazy, believe me, I've always spent an entire day with the one thought, "You're crazy, you're crazy, you're crazy," on repeat in my head. And I've heard that if you tell yourself something enough times, you start to believe it.

Well, I'm starting to question it; that's for sure.

I tighten my hold around Scarlett's small waist, feeling her ribs beneath the shirt as they rub against my forearms. She'll never worry again. She'll never lack anything again. "I swear I'll take care of you," I say, pressing a kiss against her forehead.

People will probably think I'm too young for this. I'm almost twenty-one, but I know the stereotype of people my age. Drink, party, and fuck, but I grew up with that. I've seen things, I've done things; I've experienced shit no one else has, and I think that makes me a little bit older than twenty.

I know when I have something good. Scarlett is good, too good, but I want to grow old with her. I want to spend my life with someone who gets me because I don't get me, and I need someone there to love me when I really fucking hate myself.

I bury my hand in the back of her hair, cupping her skull, and bring her closer, somehow. I squeeze my eyes shut and shake, never wanting to let her go. I feel so much better inside and out when I get to touch her.

She's light at the end of my long, windy, dark, fucked-six-ways-to-Sunday tunnel.

Placing one last kiss on her forehead, I try to pull away, but she tightens her grip around me. Soon I find myself on my back with her head resting on my chest. She mumbles something again, and it's fucking adorable. She says my name, and I hold my breath so the rise and fall of my chest doesn't wake her.

Is she dreaming of me?

"Boomer," she says my name through a sleepy giggle. "So beautiful," Scarlett sighs.

I release my breath slowly when I hear her words. I don't understand them. No one has ever thought of me as beautiful. I know I'm not, so however she sees me isn't real. I'm no good for anyone.

"Boomer," she says again. "My Boom," Scarlett mumbles, trying to bury her face in my chest again. My heart trips and falls over itself, and a small piece of my darkness turns to light. The constant intrusive thoughts slow and come to a stop.

Clarity. I'm not sure how long it will last, but however long I have, I want to spend it holding the woman I'm falling quickly in love with.

Her Boom.

I like that. I want to be her everything.

"What are you doing to me, Scarlett?" I whisper over the top of her head, running my fingers through the raven black hair. She's so perfect, everything I've ever dreamed of. It's like someone reached into my head and plucked her from my imagination, then sculpted and carved her out of the finest silk just for me.

Scarlett is a gift, a fucking present, but for what? I don't deserve to unwrap her, to smile when she bares herself to me when the time is right.

I don't care.

I'll have her anyway.

I wrap my arm around her and roll her off me until she is on her side. I need to get up. I need to go talk to Wolf. Thirty minutes have gone by, and I need information on the club. I'm also debating calling home and seeing if a few guys, including Doc, will come out, but if I do that, the risk of going back home is greater.

It's so fucking hard leaving her. Is this what it's like with people who are in love? I need to get up, but I can't. I just keep running my fingers through her inky hair and stare at her face. Her lips part while she dreams, and another giggle escapes her. She's an active sleeper, and I find it so endearing. I want to watch her forever, take note of all of her idiosyncrasies, and relive them for the rest of my life.

"Boomer," she says my name like I'm trying to get frisky with her, and I lift a brow, waiting to hear what comes next, but of course, I don't get to hear any of the good stuff. The tease. I'm left hanging. Just what is this woman dreaming about?

Gathering her hair, I slide it over her shoulder and reveal the creamy flesh of her neck. The pulse of her heart beats beneath the skin, *da dum, da dum, da dum.* I lean down and press an open-mouth kiss to the precious beat.

So warm, so soft, so sweet—so mine.

I slip my arm from under her and take my time rolling off the bed to make sure I don't wake her. She rolls back over to me, rolling on top of the arm I tried to get free of her, and she grabs onto it tight, like a monkey.

My fingers run through my hair and then I scratch the side of my head, wondering how the hell I'm going to get out of this. She's making this much harder than I thought it would be. I snag the pillow I sleep on and press it against her hand that's latched to my arm like a leech.

I love it.

Her hand finally lets go of me, and she grabs the pillow, tucking it all the way to her body. She lays her cheek against the soft cushion, just like she did my chest, and sighs in content. I finally get off the bed, stand, and stretch. When I look at the time, another fifteen minutes have gone by, and I shake my head. This girl is always going to make me lose track of time.

That's alright. I'm no longer in a hurry to change my life. Time has brought me where I needed to be, and now if the clocks wanted, they could stop ticking just so I can be with Scarlett without the worry of never having enough time.

Fuck, alright, if I don't get out of here now, I'm going to crawl back into bed with her and forget my responsibilities. I open the drawer of the nightstand next to the bed and grab my gun. It's a nine-millimeter; nothing too fancy. It's simple and effective. It does the job right. I shove it into the waistband of my shorts, under my shirt so it's well hidden, and make my way out the door.

I lock it behind me and push the key in my pocket when I'm done. The wind is cool from the sea, and it makes me relax, but not enough to stop the thoughts. Now that I'm not near her, the incessant thoughts are roaring back.

You're worthless. Stupid. It will stop if you kill yourself. Just do it. No one would care. No one would miss you.

I argue with myself, pressing my hands against my forehead, and tell myself it's not true and that I'd never kill myself, ever.

But the thoughts mock me, playing over and over again on a vicious loop.

Think of Scarlett. Think of her.

I bring up an image up of her, her beautiful body, her kind smile, her long hair, the way she says my name in her sleep, and my mind eases. The cruel thoughts slow down until they're nothing but a faint whisper in the back of my mind.

Now that I have my shit together, barely, I make my way down the steps of the piece of shit porch, and my boots sink into the sand as I make my way to the other side of the motel to see Wolf. Out of the corner of my eye, I see a shadow.

It could be my imagination. It's dark, and my mind could be playing tricks on me, but with the threat of the Ruthless Kings and their vengeance to find out whoever blew up their clubhouse circulating around the city, I can't take too many chances. I have to protect Scarlett at all costs.

I get my gun out and press my back against the wall. Wolf comes out the door, and when he makes eye contact, I lift my finger to my mouth to tell him to be quiet. He reaches behind him and pulls out his own weapon. The silver of the handle shines off the moonlight, and I appreciate the piece in his hand. It's much bigger than my nine-millimeter. One shot from that thing, and it would blow someone's fucking brains out.

"What is it?" Wolf whispers.

"Thought I saw someone," I say, cutting the corner into the poorly lit hallway. It's another thing I need to add to the list of things to repair in this place. I creep forward, keeping my gun in front of me. All I can see is the other end. The moon is so bright, casting its light on the parking lot and making it easy to see. I keep going, my boots as silent as a well-known killer. Wolf being as big as he is, is as quiet as a mouse, surprisingly having my six.

For a Ruthless King out of Atlantic City, he isn't so bad.

I come out of the other end of the hallway, surveying the area I look left and right, my gun out in front of me at the ready, and that's when I see someone leaning against my bike.

"You better get off my fucking bike before I blow your damn brains out," I seethe through clenched teeth. I can only see a slight silhouette of the person and a glowing ember dot appears in the dark, telling me he's smoking. I cock my gun, letting the click of a bullet sliding into place grab the man's attention.

He chuckles. "You sure you want to do that?" The smoke billows from his lips, disappearing into the sky. The man turns to face me, and the light hits him just right so I can see his face.

I knew his voice sounded familiar.

"Badge, what the fuck are you doing here?" I lower my weapon, and Wolf does the same.

"You know this guy?" Wolf asks.

"Yeah, I fucking know him." Fuck, this isn't good at all. "What are you doing here, Badge?"

"I came here to talk," he says, and that's when I notice he is wearing his cut. Wolf takes notice too.

"Holy shit. The Vegas chapter? You're from the original chapter? What the fuck, man? Why didn't you say anything?"

"Because it isn't important right now. Badge, I need you to take that fucking cut off now."

"How about you show me inside? You and I can talk. You explain yourself and tell me why I don't need to drag you home?"

I feel eyes on us, and the hair on the back of my neck stands up. I narrow my eyes at Badge. "Who the hell did you bring?"

"Who the hell do you think?" he says.

How am I supposed to know?

"Long time no see, Boomer." Tongue's slow drawl echoes from the darkness, but his face is nowhere to be seen.

"Who was that?" Wolf says, looking around in the dark.

Tongue's villainous laugh makes my skin shiver. "I'm a friend."

"He doesn't sound like a friend."

"He is, Wolf. I grew up with these guys. They're fine. Tongue, show yourself. You're creeping Wolf out."

I jump when a hand lands on my shoulder. "Good to see you."

"Fucking hell! You need to stop doing that."

"Why? Takes the fun out of everything," he says.

Badge flicks the cigarette to the ground and blows the rest of the smoke out of his mouth. "Enough with the pleasantries. Show us inside, and tell us what the hell is going on, and why you found the need to have your sister cry nonstop because you won't answer your phone. She thinks you're dead, Boomer."

"Is she okay?" Guilt eats away at me like a damn parasite, knowing I hurt her so much.

"You don't want to know the truth. Let's just say, I don't know if Reaper will ever forgive you for what has happened." Badge takes a step into the hallway, and I grab his arm to stop him.

"What does that mean?" Sweat, panic, and pure fear grip me. "What does that fucking mean!" I say a bit louder, and Tongue pushes me toward the hallway. He goes to open the office door when I stop him. "I get I hurt you guys, but please take the cuts off. I'll explain everything. Please," I say, hoping like hell the other chapter didn't see them roll into town.

Fuck.

This just got really messy, and I have no idea how I'm going to clean it up.

CHAPTER TWELVE

Boomer

H OMER GAVE ME THE KEY TO THE FRONT OFFICE YESTERDAY. I open the door and grab a key to a room that has a double bed. "Unless you guys want a room with a single bed? I'm sure Tongue doesn't mind cuddling."

"I only cuddle with my knife," Tongue mutters evenly without taking his eyes off the silver blade.

"Right. It was a joke, Tongue," I tell him.

He tilts his head at me, clearly not understanding the joke. "It wasn't funny."

"Tough crowd," I say, trying to ease the tension between all of us.

"I don't think it's the time for jokes, Jenkins."

Jenkins. Badge doesn't call me Boomer. Damn, I must have lost that respect the moment I signed my name at the bottom of the letter I left for Sarah. I push down the disappointment and lead the guys to the room. It's near the room I'm sharing with Scarlett, and it only makes me that much more nervous that she will see the side of me I don't want her to see.

If she ever finds out I was a Ruthless King, I'll never see her again. She'll walk away from me, and I'll have no choice but to follow, to stalk, to do my best to make sure she's safe.

The rest of my life is dedicated to her, so even if she doesn't want me, she's stuck with me; even if it means me lurking in the shadows for the rest of her life.

"Watch out for the steps; they're old as fuck and need to be replaced," I warn them and jump over three steps to land on the porch. It creaks and groans under my weight, and it sways a bit from the wind blowing, but it holds.

"This fucking place is a hair away from falling to the ground. You left us for this dump?" Badge scoffs. "Man, you better have a good reason for making me find you."

"I didn't make you do a fucking thing. You came here. I didn't ask you to be here, and I sure as hell didn't ask you to bring blades of fucking glory over there." I point to Tongue, who I catch mid-lick on his knife. "Are you kidding me?"

"What? Something was on it," he says.

"Jesus Christ," I mutter, opening the door to the room. I flip the light on as Badge throws his bag on the table, and Tongue jumps onto the bed to the right, lying flat on his back, somehow keeping the knife between his teeth without hurting himself. Crazy fucking bastard. Wolf steps in behind me and shuts the door. I peek out of the white curtain to make sure we're alone. I'll know soon if the Ruthless Kings of Atlantic City saw Badge and Tongue. It's only a matter of time before they find us. "Alright, Badge. Cut to the chase. How did you find me, and what are you doing here?"

Badge slides his finger across the TV stand and curls his lip in disgust. He's obviously not happy with the room. It's from the fucking seventies, and the man running it is older than dinosaurs. It wouldn't kill Badge to be a little more understanding.

"You know, I'm surprised it's you who came here. You're usually working. You're not around much. Why do you care?"

"I might not be around, but I do plenty for the club. And I'll have you know, I'm on a month-long vacation from the force. I have to use up my days since I never do. Boss' orders." He finally takes a seat on the bed and pulls out a flask from his cut. "How the hell do you think I found you? I tracked your phone, dipshit. It isn't hard to do. Reaper told me not to bother finding you. He thinks Tongue and I are on a ride, enjoying the sights of the fucking country or some bullshit." He takes a sip, and from the smell of it I know it's Bacardi 151. That shit is strong enough to start a lawn mower; how he drinks it, I'll never know. "So I want to know why you left, and I want to know what the hell you've gotten yourself into." He slides his eyes over to Wolf and eyes his cut. "You left our chapter for another?"

"It isn't like that." I rub my hand over my face, exhausted and fucking tired of explaining myself.

Wolf shrugs off his cut, and Badge lifts his brow. "I forgot I was wearing it. I want nothing to do with this fucking chapter. Burn it for all I care."

Something inside me swirls and awakens, and Badge laughs. "Be careful what you wish for. Jenkins here loves the flame. Ain't that right?" he says, flicking his lighter just to taunt me.

"I don't care. Burn it." Wolf leans against the wall, and it takes everything in me not to reach out and do exactly what Wolf says.

"Those are big words coming from a man who declared his life to the club. You took an oath. Taking that cut off isn't as simple as that," Badge says, taking out another cigarette.

"There should be fucking exceptions, Badge," I say. "You have no idea what you've walked in on. We're at war here." I plop down in the chair and tap my knuckles against the table. "The AC chapter, they aren't good, Badge. They bring disrespect to the Ruthless Kings' name. I have four girls here who were going to be used up and then sold. They were chained in the basement of the clubhouse like fucking animals, shackled by their hands and feet, even a collar around their neck." I motion to my neck with my hand.

"What the fuck did you just say?" Tongue sits up and stabs the nightstand, perching the knife he made into the wood.

"What you're saying is big. You know what happens if you aren't telling the truth, and you take down another chapter," Badge informs. "Why do you care? I thought MC life was beneath you, boy?"

"It wasn't about that. You don't understand, and I'm not going to waste my time explaining."

"What he's saying is true." Wolf speaks up from behind me. "I took care of the girls the best I could, but the Prez here … they're cruel sons of bitches, and this isn't the first time they've done something like this," Wolf explains. Tongue throws his blade, and I can hear the air slicing as it spins, heading right toward Wolf. It thuds into the wall next to his head, and Wolf is wide-eyed and starts to panic.

"You knew?" Tongue is in front of Wolf in no time. Tongue never misses when it comes to throwing his knife. I know he's only playing with Wolf. He yanks the sharp steel out of the wall and holds it against Wolf's throat. "You knew, and you did nothing. Why shouldn't I cut your throat now and bathe in your blood?"

Wolf doesn't say anything, and that only pisses Tongue off more.

"Tell me!" he roars, and spit flies into Wolf's face.

"Tongue, it's fine," I say, warily stepping toward him like he's a bear ready to attack. I need to be careful, or I might get a knife to the throat. "The club blackmailed him. They said if he didn't do what he was told, they would take his sister and do the same thing they do to the girls they kidnap. They killed his mom when he disobeyed the first time. He only did what he thought was best to protect his sister. He made the girls stay, as unpleasant as it was, better than what it would have been had they been in anyone else's care. He did his best," I explain. I want Tongue to lower the knife. The tip of it is piercing Wolf's neck, and a dribble of blood rolls down, pooling on his shirt.

"That true?" Tongue grunts, licking his lips as he stares at his weapon against another man's skin. He wants to cut Wolf. I can see the desire to inflict pain in Tongue's eyes. I have yet to meet someone who scares me as much as Tongue does.

Wolf nods, wincing when the knife pushes into his neck from the movement. It doesn't go in deep, but enough to make more blood come out.

Tongue removes the knife and wipes it on his jeans. He nods at Badge, and Badge lets out a long, 'This is bad' breath. Badge runs his palm over his shaved head, the fuzz sounding like sandpaper. "This isn't good. You know I have to call Reaper. I have to call in the club. What did you do; what happened? I need to know everything," Badge says, slipping off his cut and shoving it in the drawer. Tongue follows his lead, hiding the fact that they're MC. "And I want to know why I have to take off my cut."

"These girls, they don't need to be reminded. And Scarlett, if she were to..." I keep my mouth shut, and Badge nods in understanding. "You haven't told her. Makes sense with what she's been through. What all the girls have been through. How did you know to find them? I'm assuming the Prez didn't just invite you inside."

I shake my head. "No. I had no idea how much trouble they were in until Abigale, the girl who had been there the longest, showed up here at the hotel."

"I dropped her off." Wolf speaks up. "It was Scarlett's idea, one of the other girls. Abigale was really sick, and Scarlett pointed out that the Prez might not like it if one girl got the other sick, but I had to make it believable. I was already on thin ice. Scarlett suggested I shoot Abigale, and Abigale agreed. I shot her in the shoulder and carried her out of the clubhouse. Homer, the guy who owns this place, I heard good things about him. I thought she'd be safe here. Abigale was the only chance for the girls to be found."

"Abigale told me of their schedules and how they're gone most of the morning and afternoon. I scoped out the place, and she was right. I made my way in and rescued all the girls. After, I may or may not have thrown a grenade..."

Tongue cackles, sounding like a hyena. Badge pinches the bridge of his nose and curses. "Doing that caused war, Jenkins."

"Something that should've been started years ago," Wolf states, pushing off the wall. "I don't know how many women they've done this to, but they don't just sell them. They rape them, drug them, use them, beat them, and if they're too far gone, they kill them and burn the bodies so they can never be found. This entire city is afraid to cross the Ruthless Kings."

I nod, thinking about how Homer said he still pays them. "They take most of Homer's money. It's why this place is such a shithole. They killed his wife too."

Badge's eyes swirl with anger. Tongue flips his blade in his hand, and I know they're itching to take these fuckers down and disband this chapter. "We have to let Reaper know, Jenkins. You know all the chapters answer to him since Vegas is where it all started. If this is going on, he has to know."

Which means Reaper and the rest of the MC will come into town, guns fucking blazing. "Can you just give me some time before you do that, please?" I need to somehow find the courage to tell Scarlett the truth about me, about where I'm from, who raised me.

"Only because Reaper and Sarah need their time before this bullshit slaps them in the face."

"Why? What happened?"

"Sarah had a miscarriage a few hours after she read your letter. Believe me when I say you're the last person Reaper wants to see, hear from, or think about. He told the entire chapter not to call you Boomer anymore if we were to speak to you again. He's pissed. Sarah isn't well. She's in bed, depressed, and hasn't moved for days."

Worthless. Stupid. It's all your fault. Kill yourself. You're no good for anybody. They'll be better off.

I grip my head when the thoughts take control again, and tears sting the back of my eyes. Over and over, non-stop on a loop, and I can't take it anymore. I run out the door, blaming myself for ruining my sister's life, and I head right toward the ocean.

Hoping like hell it swallows me up and never spits me out.

CHAPTER THIRTEEN

Scarlett

I WAKE UP TO THE SOUND OF SHOUTING IN THE DISTANCE. I ROLL over, expecting to feel Boomer when cold sheets awaken my skin, causing me to finally open my eyes. The room is empty, and the cold dread of panic sets in. I'm alone. He left me alone.

The clock flashes one in the morning, and I push myself up, the mattress giving from my weight under my hands. I rub the sleep out of my eyes and get out of bed. My bladder is full, so I sleepily stumble into the bathroom to relieve myself. I wash my hands, splash some cold water on my face to wake up, and pat my face dry with a hand towel hanging to the left on the silver handle. I take a good look at myself. I have a few bruises on my face, my cheeks are a bit chapped still, but I'm healing quickly. I guess it helps that I'm not sitting in a puddle of filth.

I hang the towel up and walk into the room, wondering where Boomer is. All of his stuff is still here, and I know he wouldn't ever leave me. More shouts, frantic and loud, catch my attention. I take a chance and move the curtain slightly to see a few men I don't recognize running toward the water.

Then I see Wolf running after them.

Fear grips me, telling me that something is very wrong. I don't bother putting on pants, not when his shirt comes to my knees. I unlock the door and fling it open, smashing it against the wall by accident. It leaves a dent, and a few pieces of drywall hit the ground, but I don't care. The wood of the porch is cold and grainy from the sand.

It doesn't seem like anything could be wrong. The beach is deserted, the stars are out, and the waves crash against the shore musically. It's relaxing. A total contradiction to how these men are acting.

I jump off the porch and land in the sand, nearly sinking, and bolt. I pump my arms when I hear one of them yell "Jenkins" into the empty water. I think of the worst. No, this can't be happening. He wouldn't ever leave me, not like this. Then again, I don't really know Boomer, do I? I know him as the savior, not as the man, and maybe the torment I saw in him earlier has everything to do with why one man is diving into the ocean while the other wades out until the water is to his neck.

I pump my arms faster, and my breath is hard to come by. I'm already getting winded. "What's wrong? What's happening?" I shout at Wolf, who's currently pacing up and down the shoreline calling for Boomer. "Wolf!" I tug on his arm to get his attention.

"I-I don't know. Boomer just got some really bad news,

and before we knew it, he ran into the ocean. We don't know where he went."

I turn to the vast sea, the ugly slick tendrils of fear gripping my heart. The water looks black, a large oil-colored pool where unknown oddities lurk. He can be anywhere. I've never been in the ocean before, but I'm willing to go in there for him. He saved me. The least I can do is be there for him.

"Boomer!" I scream out at the same time as a man calls for him. "Boomer, please!" I cry, pushing the water apart as if that will help, hoping I see something of the man that I'm growing to depend on. "Boomer, where are you?"

"Boomer," the tall, scary man with murderous eyes says slowly, but loud enough to make me start looking in a different section of the water. I'm afraid the man might drown me if I get in his way.

"I got him!" another guy with a shaved head swims out further to a long figure floating in the water.

I cup my hands over my mouth and shake my head. "No! No, Boomer!" I'm about to dive into the water and swim out there myself to hold Boomer in my arms, to cradle him, to tell him he can't leave me; not like this. Whatever is happening, I'll be there for him. I'll guide him, whatever I have to do.

He just needs to give me the chance to do it.

Wolf wraps his arms around me when the stranger swims forward, guzzling saltwater as he pulls Boomer behind him.

"Boomer." His name is a long, broken sob leaving my lips, and the hope I felt is replaced by devastation. What can he despise so much that he wanted to end his life? Am I not enough? Aren't the people who love him enough? "Let go of me." I try to thrash out of Wolf's hold when the stranger lifts Boomer into his arms, and the water cascades down them in sheets as he gets to his feet on the ocean floor and begins to walk.

"No. You don't need to see this," Wolf says.

"Let. Me. Go!" I seethe and ram my elbow into Wolf's stomach. I try to walk toward the two men I've never met before. Boomer lays limp in a pair of arms, hair dripping with water and his eyes are shut.

Even in death he looks so beautiful. His jaw catches the moonlight, and his shirt sticks to his body; this time it isn't appealing. Not when his chest isn't moving, and his hazel eyes aren't on me.

The waves try to suck me back, the tide strong and relentless. The damn ocean is a murderer in itself. It's beautiful, sure, but it's violent, and it isn't afraid to show its rage. I won't let something as simple as water stop me from getting to Boomer. I lift my knee to my chest and heavily pound my feet into the waves to get to the shore. Boomer's shirt is weighing me down since it is wet. My lungs burn, and my skin starts to tingle where the salt is causing the wounds to open again.

Boomer is laid on the sand, and the scary one pushes the other guy out of the way and leans down to see if he can hear a heartbeat.

He shakes his head.

"Oh, god!" I finally get to Boomer, his lifeless body, and I fall next to him. I push his wet hair back and rub his face. "You can't leave me like this," I tell him.

"Tongue, tilt his head back. Do CPR."

Tongue, if that's even his real name, does as the other man says and blows three breaths into Boomer's mouth. His chest expands, then deflates.

On repeat.

And then one palm over the other, Tongue starts compressions. He's counting, shaking his head with doubt when there are no signs of improvement.

"You have to save him," I whisper.

"I'm not letting my family die," Tongue continues to press against Boomer's chest, and I swear I hear something crack. I reach for Tongue to tell him to stop and that he's doing more harm than good, but Wolf pulls me away.

"He's hurting him! Let me go! Let me go, Wolf! I swear to god! I'll kill you if you don't let me go," I scream hysterically, watching as what was a life-saving measure turns into something cruel. "They're hurting him."

"It's normal," Wolf says. "It's supposed to be intense. Sometimes ribs crack."

Tears pool in my eyes as I watch Tongue fight to save Boomer. His long hair falls in his face, dripping with saltwater and sand.

"You don't get to fucking die like this. Not after everything..." Tongue lifts his hands in the air and balls them into fists.

I don't have enough time to stop him. He's bringing his arms down at a fast, alarming rate, and when his fist collides with Boomer's chest, the pain radiates to me and I gasp, collapsing in the sand as I wait for that sharp inhale from Boomer's lips.

He can't leave me. Where would I go? I don't want to live a life without him. I've had that life before, and it did nothing for me. Boomer is the rejuvenation my soul needs. If he leaves me now, I'll only be the girl who was taken, not the girl who was saved.

I'm only saved when Boomer breathes.

A small cough sounds, and Boomer rolls to his side, throwing up a ton of water. He lays his head in the sand and struggles to breathe. I crawl over to him on hands and knees, not caring how bad it hurts my wounds, and I cradle his head.

Tongue falls back to his ass and stares up at the sky. He looks exhausted from the exertion and endurance it took.

"You stupid fuck."

I rip my gaze up to the man whose name I don't know, and I'm about to open my mouth to tell him off when Tongue shakes his head. "Not now, Badge."

Badge? What the hell kind of names are these.

"No! You stupid fuck. You tried to kill yourself? After what your sister has already gone through? Are you kidding me? Are you trying to kill her?" Badge yells, picking Boomer up by his wet shirt and ripping him from my lap.

Boomer's agonizing cry rips through the air at the pain from his beat-up ribs. He's still coughing and sputtering water, those luminous hazel eyes of his barely blinking. I can live with that. Just as long as his chest rises and falls with life, I'm alright.

Badge's voice chokes. "Do you have any idea what would happen to Reaper? To us? To the men who watched you grow. You're fucking family." He shakes Boomer. "Family! Are you trying to drive us insane? What the hell was that?" Badge finally breaks, bringing Boomer to his chest in a hug. "You have no idea how much we need you or how much you're loved. What the fuck is going on with you, boy? Huh? What is it? Talk to us. We're here, Boomer. We're here."

I can't see Boomer's face, but his hands tighten on Badge's shirt, squeezing the water out.

"You can't do that." Badge lowers Boomer to the ground

and cups his face. "You hear me? Do you get that? Do you know how many people love you? Answer me."

"No," Boomer gasps. "No. I didn't think anyone would care if I was gone."

Badge cups the back of Boomer's head and lays it on his chest. "You're wrong, boy. You're wrong. If that isn't enough, look at that girl over there. She about took down Wolf to get to you. And those tears, they aren't fake. If you're looking for a declaration of love, she's standing right there."

Boomer stumbles, gripping on to Badge as he takes a step forward, his eyes finally wide and alert as he stares at me.

Energy crackles and zings between us, and he does his best to walk to me, but he falls, cradling his ribs. I run to him and catch him, letting him rest his head against my shoulder. "I'm sorry, sugar," he says, lifting his head. His forehead leans against mine, and I hold onto him tight, making sure nothing can ever take him from me again. "Never again," he promises and kisses my cheek.

I was more afraid tonight than I was in those bikers' basement as a captive. I think it's because my life was over, and I came to terms with it, but then Boomer rescued me and gave me hope, and I was ready to be alive again; ready for something amazing to drown out the nightmare of what I experienced.

It's fucked up. I should care more about my life, I suppose, but ideas change when the end is facing you. I truly believe every end has a beginning now.

And Boomer is mine.

CHAPTER FOURTEEN

Boomer

MY CHEST FEELS LIKE SHIT. TONGUE REALLY WENT FULL FORCE on the CPR. I'm thankful, but my god. It's been three days, and it still hurts like a motherfucker. No one has left my side, and to be honest, it's pissing me off. I didn't actually mean to drown myself. I don't think I did. I don't know. Fuck, I really have no idea. I didn't want to die, but I wanted the thoughts to stop, just for a second.

Especially after what Badge told me. The thoughts tripled, sending me into a downward spiral, and I only wanted peace. I realized how much I fucked up after I dove into the water, and the current took me. I wanted to live, I just… I don't know what happened. I guess I gave up, and that isn't a good enough reason. I should've been stronger because Scarlett needs me and, in that moment, I failed her.

Right now, she's with Homer and Wolf. They went to

the next state over to take the girls to a hospital to make sure they're alright. After I get the go-ahead from Scarlett's doctor, I'm going to make my move.

"Get the fuck out of the way, Badge."

Oh. Fuck.

No.

Nope.

That's not who I think it is.

"Reaper, don't go in there guns blazing, okay? He just—"

"I know what the hell he did." Reaper's voice carries loudly from behind the door, pissed off and sounding like he wants to kill.

"Reaper," Badge tries to calm him again, but then the door is kicked in by a huge size fifteen boot, ripping the old, cheap wood off its hinges.

"Shit," I say, rolling off the bed into a standing position. I feel like a kid again, getting in trouble for starting trash can fires, but it's more now. Reaper has invested in me, and I'm more than some kid now—I'm his kid. What I did, leaving and then almost drowning... He's going to unleash his fury on me.

"Jenkins," he growls, stomping toward me with pure anger in his eyes, the promise of blood and revenge coming off him in waves. He stops in front of me, wide chest heaving as he grips my shirt with his fists. He shakes me a bit, unsure of what he wants to do with me. His jaw tics, and his eyes flip from anger to relief, sadness, and betrayal. Reaper thought he was good at hiding his emotions, but I knew better. He let them show on his face more than he let on.

I prepare myself for a punch in the face, for the worst beatdown of my life, but Reaper's dark eyes well with tears, and he sniffles, yanking me to his chest so hard the breath escapes my lungs. A bit of pain makes me gasp, but I stand still as Reaper holds me.

Crying.

Reaper's a big man, bigger than most of the guys in the MC. I'm not a small man either and, right now, I feel like a dwarf.

His body shakes and with slow, tentative moves, I lift my arms and tighten them around the man who took care of me most of my life. I'm a selfish fuck. I should've never left home, but then I wouldn't have found Scarlett, so I don't regret anything.

The hard thuds of other boots coming into the room has me lifting my gaze. Tool is there, brushing his beard with his fingers, then Knives, Bullseye, and Poodle. Poodle is whistling, glancing anywhere but at me and Reaper. Bullseye and Tool are looking right at me, and they don't look as relieved as Reaper is.

I'm starting to wonder if I'm going to get that punch.

"What the fuck, kid?" Reaper leans back, and when I look at his face, I don't see tears, but his eyes are red. "What the fuck!" he roars, shoving me with his hands.

There it is.

"You're going to do that to me? To us? Just what the hell is wrong with you?"

I want to answer him, if only I knew how. My mental state was slowly getting worse when I left Vegas, but finding Scarlett gave me hope, a reason to live.

It can't be on her to fix me. I need to fix myself. As easy as it is to just let myself be and have her carry the burden, I can't because I'm a better man than that. I'd like to think I am, at least. Last night doesn't prove it, but I can be better.

"What about your sister? What about your dad? You think your dad would have wanted that? You scared the hell out of me when Badge called to tell me Tongue had to—" His voice chokes with emotion, and he stares down at his boots. "When Tongue had to revive you, and then to say he almost didn't... Almost, Boomer." He lets my nickname slip, and hearing it from him gives me hope. "Do you ever think I want to hear that my kid almost died?" He bangs his chest. "I just lost a fucking kid. I can't lose you too. Do you hear me? Do you fucking understand me?" He slams me against the wall and fists my shirt, picking me up until the material rips, but it doesn't give way. "Do you understand?" he asks again, and this one time a lone tear falls from Reaper's eye. Just one.

But that one speaks a million emotions, a million words.

"I understand, Reaper," I whisper and wrap my hands around his wrists. "I'm sorry."

"Fucking hell, kid." He slams me against his chest again. "I thought I had lost you to distance, but then almost losing you to death fucked me up, Boomer. You can't do shit like that."

I nod, feeling emotions bubble up in my chest. I feel like a kid again. That lost little boy who had no idea where he belonged after his dad died. "I'm sorry, Reaper. I'm fucked in the head, okay? I'm fucked up." I slam my palm against the side of my head when that little thought creeps back in, telling me that Reaper doesn't mean a word, that I'm worthless and always will be.

I always disappoint.

I always mess up.

I ruin everything.

I deserve to die.

"I'm fucked up!" I scream again, slamming my hand against

my head. "Here, right here, Reap. I'm fucked up. It won't stop. It never stops. It goes on and on and on. I left because I wanted to get better, and I didn't want to burden anyone because that's what I am. That's what I've always been. You don't think I know that?" I clutch my chest when it becomes too hard to breathe.

A shadow falls in the door, and Tongue appears, tilting his head at me like he doesn't understand why I'm freaking out.

Reaper grabs my hand from my head, stopping me from hitting myself again. "I fucked up somewhere if that's what you really think. Whatever you think is wrong, we're here for you. It's what family is for, Boomer. If you feel sick here"—he taps my head—"then you can't feel here." He presses his fingers against my heart. "You come to me. I'll help you. Do you get that? You don't leave us. You don't leave Sarah."

"Is she okay?" I ask, ripping my hand away from Reaper and making my way to sit on the bed. I grab Scarlett's pillow and inhale. The shampoo she used the night before lingers, and my mind slowly stops torturing me. "Is she here? I want to see her," I ask Reaper through cloudy eyes as I bring the pillow down to my lap.

Reaper shakes his head. "No. I didn't want her to make the trip. She's going through something personal. A few of the guys held back and stayed with her. She's in good hands."

"And she's mad as fuck at you and didn't want to make the trip," Tool says, flipping the screwdriver in his hand.

"Tool!" Reaper scolds.

"What? It's true. All of us are pissed, and while I feel for whatever you're going through, what you did wasn't right."

"I know. I know that," I say solemnly and rub the pillow with my hand. "You don't get it. The club was never everything to me, and I needed to figure out why."

"Did you?" Tool asks.

"I'm working on it." I look at all of them and notice they aren't wearing their cuts. Reaper must see my shock. and he sits next to me, releasing a heavy sigh.

"Badge told us the story. The last thing we want is to give any of the girls here panic. I also want to know more about this chapter. In order to do that, you and I need to go in and see exactly what they're up to."

I stand in a rush and look at everyone, shaking my head. "No." I go to hit my head again and remember who I'm in front of. I can't do that in front of them; it's why they never knew. "No, it'll be too late for that. These guys are assholes, Reaper. We can't wait. Let's just go in there and kill them. I'll blow that fucking clubhouse up."

"Send me," Tongue says from another corner of the room.

He was just in the doorway. What the fuck. Maybe it isn't me who needs my head examined.

"Tongue, not now," Reaper says, holding his hand up to stop Tongue from saying anything else.

Tongue steps forward, and that's when I see point studs on his boots, ready to do some damage. "We can send a message to them."

"I already did that, and for some reason, they haven't come here yet. They've stayed in the city."

"But I want to," Tongue says, his voice slightly whiny.

Reaper ignores him, rubbing his tired eyes. Tool sits in the chair by the round table and studies the room. "This would be nice if it wasn't so old."

"I'm going to help Homer redo it. Ruthless Kings have stolen enough from him."

"The old man in the office?" Poodle asks, staring out of the curtain at the ocean. "This is such a pretty view. I can see why he wants to keep it."

"Pretty view?" Tool looks over the mountain of his shoulder. "What are you? An agent from HGTV?"

"Why do you even know that channel?" Poodle spins around and points a finger. "It's because you watch it too!"

"Do not!" Tool stands, and the chair falls to pieces at his feet, crumbling into chunks of firewood.

"Do too! That's the only way. Tell 'em, Bullseye."

"Shut up, Poodle," Bullseye says. "It doesn't matter."

"Okay, can we all shut up and get to the point of the problem? There are a few here, and we only have so much time. It's late." Reaper stares at the time on his phone. "I need to call Sarah; she's probably worried out of her mind. We've been on the road for days."

"We'll talk tomorrow, but there's one person I'm sending in here tonight before the girls get back."

"Is this not everyone with you?" I ask, peering around the room.

"No. We brought Doc. He quit his job at the hospital, and now he works for us full-time. We told him what was going on, and he offered to come."

"Why would you bring Doc in here?" There's nothing physically wrong with me, and it will be a waste of Doc's time to check me.

"So you can talk to him about this." Reaper taps his temple, and immediately I feel like less of a man. I feel crazy.

"No, fuck that. I'm fine. I didn't ask for that." I throw the pillow on the floor and stand. "No. Get out. Out! Get the fuck out! All of you."

Tool takes two steps in front of me, lifts his fist in the air, and swings. His knuckles hit my chin, and I stagger, slamming against the wall as I cup my jaw. I swear to God I see the fucking future with how hard he hit me. "What the hell was that for?"

"That's for being an insensitive asshole. We drove four days to get here. Four fucking days. Your sister miscarried. The club has been up in arms about you, and you know what? I'm fucking sick of it. Get your shit together, stop acting like a spoiled little bitch, and get the fuck over yourself. You obviously need help, so get help, so you can be a better man to Scarlett because who you are won't fucking work. And if you won't be a better man, I can be the one she needs. I hear she's a pretty little thing."

I lift my fist and let it fly. Of course, Tool is superhuman, and it would take a rocket to make him move. I slam my fist against his jaw, and he hardly blinks. "You won't go near her."

"Then get your shit together, and maybe I won't have to," he snarls, bringing his head down to mine. "Reaper might have open arms when it comes to you, Jenkins, but I fucking don't. You're twenty. You're a man. It's time you start thinking like one." Since Tool is the VP, everyone listens to him too. He whistles and stomps out the door, kicking the other half of the porch down as he makes his wrathful path.

One by one the others follow him out, and the only person left with me is Reaper. Since the door is open, well broken, the cold breeze makes its way in. "I came here wanting to say a lot of things, kid." Reaper stands, and the chains around his pockets jiggle together as he glances around. "I was mad—fuck, I was mad—and when I had to hold my wife when she miscarried, balling her eyes out, I wanted to kill you, Boomer. I'd never wanted to kill you before, but I wanted to kill you for only adding to her pain. It isn't your fault she miscarried. It was an ectopic pregnancy. There was no chance for the baby, but I blamed you. I ignored everything Badge told me about your situation, and I zeroed in on the fact that I knew where you were. You left, like a coward, not even able to face me. It was a spit in the face after everything you and I have been through." He stops in front of the worn, secondhand dresser and stares at the photo I have of us fishing. "And then I remembered I'm allowed to be mad and disappointed in my kid, and I know I'd never kill you but, Boomer—"

"Reaper—"

"No, don't. You're still young; you're still a kid. You have a lot to learn about life still. So tell me about Scarlett," Reaper says, keeping his back to me as he stares so hard at the picture. I wonder if he's reliving the memory in his head.

"She was in bad shape, but I got to her in time. She's strong, beautiful, and a bit shy considering the circumstances. I want her as mine."

"It's a big label. If you were in the club, would you make her your ol' lady?"

"I would. I knew from the moment I saw her."

Reaper reaches into the side of his bag he threw down when he kicked in the door and pulls out the one thing that meant the world to me, and I left it behind. "That's yours, kid. It was your father's. Sarah doesn't want it." He tosses it to me, and I unfold it, placing it in my lap. The prospect patch has been replaced with a newer patch that says 'member.' I glance up at him in confusion, rubbing my hand along the patch. I don't understand. I've done nothing to deserve this.

"You prospected enough, kid," he says. "Your entire life was the club. You lost your father to the club; you nearly gave your life for the club, and your sister. You were done prospecting a long time ago, and I should have just patched you in. It's yours if you want it."

"Reaper," I start to say, but my throat tightens.

"You don't have to answer now," he says. "Hide it from your ol' lady. I think you're meant to be a part of something bigger than just you. You aren't alone, okay? I'll send Doc in. I need to go call Sarah." Before I can say anything else, Reaper practically runs out the door, leaving me staring at a cut I never thought I'd see again.

My chest hurts, but it isn't from being brought back to life; it's the sudden love I feel from everyone, especially when all I deserve is hate.

CHAPTER FIFTEEN

Scarlett

"**S**OMEONE HAS HEARTS IN THEIR EYES," JOANNA TEASES AS we speed down the highway next to the ocean. It's so pretty here. I'd hate to leave. I might have been in a basement and never explored the place, but from what I've seen—the big casinos, the ocean, the motel—I like it. It's better than the small town I'm from where everyone knows everyone, and if I went back there, everyone would point, stare, and whisper, and I don't want to live like that.

"I don't know what you mean," I mumble, turning to look out the window to stare at nothing. I'm hiding my smile from Joanna, Melissa, and Abigale. They're all staring at me in the back of this beat-up Bronco, and Homer's eyes keep flicking in the rearview. Wolf has his hand reaching on the other side of the seat by the door, and Abigale has her hand in his.

Like we can't tell.

Right.

"It wouldn't have to do with that little dipshit staying with me, is it?" Homer asks, pushing his big square seventies style glasses up his nose. "I'll give him a talking to."

"Oh, I know you would." I lean forward and pinch his cheeks. Homer is the cutest old man I have ever freaking seen. And sweet, so damn sweet. I'm not sure what we would do without him.

"It's Boomer, right?" Melissa says in a low whisper. She's been very quiet this entire time. Everyone handles trauma differently, but I can tell she's trying to be better. Every word she speaks, everywhere she looks, she's waiting for them to jump out and take her again. She shakes constantly, and her anxiety makes her scratch the skin on her forearms. "You trust him?" she asks.

Thinking of Boomer, my mind reels with what might happen when I return to the motel. We aren't far away. Less than five miles, and I've been building up the courage to kiss him. I want to push my fears away and hold onto the present, enjoy the good, and relish in pleasure. I want to give myself over to Boomer and not live in fear.

Not like Melissa or Joanna. I can't. I'm not like them. I have to push it back and keep going, or I'll be miserable for the rest of my life, and I don't want to be miserable. I want to kiss his temples where his pain seems to radiate and sooth his beautiful, chaotic mind.

"Look at that blush. Girl, you aren't hiding anything," Abigale jokes, but it's soon followed with a deadly cough. The hospital wanted to keep her overnight, but she wanted to get back to the motel. I think right now, that's where all of us feel safe.

As we pass a few trees that are burnt from lightning, Homer takes a right, and two minutes following the road along the beach, we pull into the hotel to see a bunch of bikes parked.

Melissa grips my hand, and Joanna grabs hers along with Abigale's. We're locked like a chain. Wolf turns to look back at us, his blue eyes taking on a murderous hue. "Get down. Get as low to the floorboard as you can. Lay flat."

"What is this hootenanny shit? I told him not to throw parties," Homer mutters, and I know he's just trying to make us feel better. The claws of panic dig into my chest, and I gasp for breath. They're here. Fuck, they're here. I don't want to go back. Please, god, don't make me go back.

"I'm going to check things out. I'll be back," Wolf says as he climbs out of the vehicle.

"Wolf!" Abigale scrambles for his hand. "Wolf, no!" But it's too late, and he's on his way inside. She breaks down and cries, burying her face in her hands, and Joanna wraps her arm around Abigale, tucking her against her chest.

"Shhh, you have got to be quiet," Joanna hisses, but it's a pleading tone laced with desperation. "Please, Abigale. They'll hear you."

Abigale quietens down because I give her my hand to squeeze. She squeezes so hard my damn finger pops, and I have to swallow down a moan.

"Ladies, it's okay. Wolf just gave me the nod of approval. You're safe. Let's get everyone inside. I'll get your bags," Homer says, but none of us move.

I'm too afraid to get up.

What was it I just said? I can't live in misery. I have to do this. The moment I see Boomer, I'm going to kiss him and tell him I want him. I'm going to seize the moment because I had way too many taken away from me, and I'm not about to let it start again. "Come on. We have to go." I rip my hand from Abigale's and crawl out from behind Homer's seat. I barely have my feet on the ground when strong arms wrap around my waist, and I can't help the scream that leaves my mouth.

"Shh, it's me! It's me. Fuck, I'm sorry, sugar."

Boomer.

I turn in his arms and lay my hand on his chest, the same chest that was just crushed a few days ago, and while I know he's alive, the thump of his heart brings me so much happiness.

"What's wrong?" he asks as his big hazel eyes search my face for answers. "Scarlett?" All I can think about are his lips; lips I should've tasted the first day I saw him. "Sugar, you're scaring me; what is it? Is it the bikes? I can explain that. You're safe here."

I can't take it anymore. I jump on him, wrap my legs around his waist, and circle my arms around his neck, diving in before my moment of courage flies away. My lips meet his as the wind brushes through my hair. He doesn't hesitate; he kisses me back the moment we touch.

His lips are soft, just like I knew they would be, plump and big; they nearly take over my mouth. With one hand, he grips my jaw, controlling me and the way I move. It's gentle, but it's a touch that has me whimpering into his mouth. Boomer takes the small opportunity of space and slides his tongue between my lips. The lingering taste of beer on his taste buds entices my tongue to dance with his, gathering all the flavor I can.

My back hits the Bronco, and Boomer's hands fall to my ass, holding me up by my globes. Hoots and hollers cheer somewhere in the distance, and I'm surprised that being watched is only turning me on. I dig my nails into his neck and moan down his throat. I ache to feel him inside me.

He grinds his hard cock against me and yanks away, cursing, "Fuck, sugar. You sure are a bomb of surprises." His eyes fall to my mouth, my lips tingling from our passionate kiss, and my body throbs with need. I try to grind against him again, but he stops me, closing his eyes as his body shakes to pull himself together.

I did that.

I made him lose control like that.

Boomer is intricate, delicate, just like the bombs he loves so much. I'm the match to his fuse, and now all that's left is the explosion building between us.

"You better stop looking at me like that, Scarlett, or I'll fuck you right here in front of everyone," he growls, those hazel eyes swirling again with a tint of danger that only makes my body grow more curious for him.

I moan at the thought of someone watching us, and Boomer lays his head on my shoulder. "You're killing me, sugar. You pretend to be all soft and sweet, but you're a fucking savage, aren't you?"

"I've been wanting to taste your lips for too long," I say, suddenly feeling a bit embarrassed. Maybe he didn't like how forward I was. Does he want soft and sweet all the time? I have a feeling that isn't who I am. He makes me feel dainty but powerful all at once; like a piece of candy, but a craving someone shouldn't give into.

"Come on. Let's take you back to the room. I want to hear about how your day went."

"Can that wait?" I ask, biting my bottom lip, and his eyes

fall to my mouth again. He licks his lips, watching me intently. "I want to keep kissing you."

He sets me down and takes my hand, dragging me behind him. We walk past a group of really big men, one with a knife who gives me a wave that a serial killer would give before swooping in to take their victim. "I'll introduce you to everyone later," Boomer says, almost tripping over the ridge in the sidewalk.

"I hear he has a little dick!" a guy with a screwdriver above his ear shouts, smiling at me. I can't tell if he's joking or not.

"Fuck you, Tool!" Boomer shouts angrily at the guy.

I won't care if Boomer is small. I like him for him. There are other ways to please a woman, and plus, I hear it only takes four inches to give a woman an orgasm. I really hope Boomer can give me one because I've never experienced it. I've had sex with one guy, and he didn't make me come.

I'm ready.

I want it.

I want to have a sex-a-thon where all we do is screw all day and night, and then do it again the next day. I want to be so tired, sore, and sweaty that I can't utter my name. Can Boomer give that to me? Small cock or not?

The hallway is dark for a moment before we break through to the other side that faces the ocean. I hate how beautiful the view is because it's a lie. The water isn't afraid to take you under, and the only way to come back up is to fight or have someone else fight for you.

It's a monster in a beautiful disguise.

When we get to the door, I notice one hinge is broken while the other one is holding the weight of the door as it leans. There's a huge hole in the middle where someone kicked it in, and I have so many questions.

Why is the door like this, and who are those men out front?

But when we get inside and Boomer throws me on the bed, I suddenly don't care anymore.

He rips his shirt off, showing the defined muscles. A large tattoo takes over his entire chest, red and black swirling through it. I don't stare at it long enough to get the full picture because my eyes trial down to his stomach.

Eight. There are eight abs and one hell of a scar. I want to lick every single one of them and scratch them as he's buried inside me.

"The door," I say, noticing it's open. Any one of his friends can walk by and see us.

"What?" he stops mid-step and gives the evil eye to the broken door.

The expression makes me giggle. It looks like he's about to light it on fire. He tries to put the door back where it belongs, but the hinges creak, and then the damn thing falls lower to the ground than it did before.

"Son of a bitch. Fucking Reaper. He had to kick the goddamn door down. Always having to make an entrance. We get it. You're big. You're fucking bad. Jesus Christ."

It's enjoyable to see him talk to himself. It's cute. Boomer's hands land on his hips, and he stares at the ceiling in frustration. He turns around, and his eyes land on the dresser. The forlorn pinch in his eyes disappears, and a smile takes over his face. He grabs the dresser and slides it across the floor until it's flush with the door. Boomer then flips the lock and surprisingly it does.

He still has his hand on the metal knob when he looks over his shoulder, and the vehement veil in his eyes cause a shiver to crawl up and down my spine. The calm and collected Boomer is gone, and the wild, unpredictable one has taken his place. He prowls toward me until he's in front of the bed, staring down at me like I'm his prey.

I am. I want him to sink his teeth into my flesh and devour. I just hope I taste so good he comes back for seconds and thirds; hell, I hope he never gets his fill.

"I'm going to tell you right now that if I kiss you again and you grind your pussy against my cock, I might not be able to stop."

"I don't want you to stop," I say, my cheeks turning a bright crimson from the flush of heat.

"You need to be sure." One of his knees lands on the bed, then the other, and he knee walks to me, and the hungry blaze in his eyes has me inching backward. He seems to like my hesitation because he grips my ankle and pulls me toward him, my back sliding easily against the simple blue cotton comforter. "You need to be sure; do you know why?"

I shake my head, unable to form words. I stare at him with so much awe, I'm sure it looks pathetic. I want to know why. I want to know everything he has to say.

"Because I haven't had sex in a really long time, sugar. I'll be honest, I was afraid my cock would never get hard for a woman again, but then you came along." He brings my leg to his mouth and places a kiss on my ankle. "And I've been fucking hard since the moment I met you. I was fucking done with the easy chicks."

The thought of him being with someone else sends me into a fit of jealousy and rage. I sit up and grip the waistband of his jeans. "No one else. No one else but me, Boomer. If we do this, it's only us and no one else."

"I'm fucked up, sugar. You don't know the half of it." The sadness is evident in his voice, and all I want to do is be the solution to all his problems, even if it's impossible.

"I want to know, Boomer. Show me," I tell him, inching toward his red, swollen lips. "Tell me everything, and I swear, I'll love you for it." His eyes snap to mine, and the shadows that invoke fear shrink back, and the man who's afraid comes forth. He's only there for a minute before he's bringing his mouth down on mine. This kiss is different.

It's slower. His lips own my entire mouth, my entire being, and both of his hands cup my face. He takes a breath and then dives back in, moaning into my mouth as if he can't get enough. The more we kiss, the more frantic he gets. I open my eyes for a split second to see what he looks like, and his brows are pinched, and his eyes are shut.

He's desperate.

He needs me.

Me.

The girl he found in a basement, chained, and almost broken.

"Boomer," I say his name, and he shakes his head.

"Don't call me that. Call me Jenkins in bed. It's who I want to be with you here. *Here* is the most important place, and you should get the most important part of me."

"And that isn't Boomer?"

He shakes his head as he trails his fingers along my neck where the iron collar was. I'll always have a slight scar. It's still healing, and I know it's ugly. I try to cover it up, but he snatches my hand and holds it against the bed. "I get to see every part of you, if you get to see all the ugly inside me," he says.

I kiss him again, soft and tender, something I expect

has never happened to him, and place my hand on his chest.

"Jenkins, when will you learn there is nothing ugly about you? I think you're beautiful."

"I'm fucking crazy, Scarlett."

"That's okay. Just be crazy *for* me."

He lays me down and hovers over me, sliding his finger along my jawline. Tiny, little sparks ignite under my skin. It takes all I have not to close my eyes and let my body feel what he's doing to me. Every part of me is affected by him. He thinks he's ruined, that he's haunted, but I want him to come closer to me. He's made himself at home in my bones, the foundation of my being, and just like a ghost, there's no way out.

"Sugar, don't you know yet? I've been crazy for you the moment I saw you."

CHAPTER SIXTEEN

Boomer

A BRIGHT CRIMSON COLOR CREEPS DOWN HER NECK FROM MY statement.

The only thing *scarlet* about Scarlett is the flush that takes over her cheeks when she wants me. If she is really ready, I'll handle her with the delicate ease she deserves, and I'll see just how far that flush really goes.

"Do you?" I ask her again, wanting to hear her say the words. I need to hear them, or I won't believe her; no matter what her body tells me.

You won't be good enough for her. You won't be able to please her. She can do better. Go back into the ocean. Spare her.

"Yes, Jenkins. I want you. I want this."

But my judgment is clouded from the thoughts. Her words are distorted as I try not to listen to my own worst enemy. I try to remember the conversation with Doc after I revealed everything that happened me with.

He calls them obsessive intrusive thoughts. They're O.C.D. tendencies and can cause severe anxiety, which might be another reason I wasn't able to get an erection for so long. He gave me medicine, and I have to take it once a day for the rest of my life. It takes two weeks to work, and I just have to keep pushing through.

"Come back to me, Jenkins."

My name falling from her lips and her hands pressing against my bare chest lift the fog. The thoughts retreat, and when I look down to see her soft palms against me, I know when I want to truly feel at my best, her hands have to be on me.

"I'm here, sugar. I'm right here." I grab her hand and bring it to my mouth, kissing the slender, precious digits. Gently, I lay her arm beside her and lift the hem of her shirt to reveal smooth skin. Some patches are still pink from where it was rubbed raw, but it's healing nicely. I inch her shirt up, revealing more of her slender body. Her rib cage comes to view and with every inhale, the bones that protect the most sacred part of her can be seen.

My hands are so big, my fingers nearly touch from how small her waist is. So fucking small. What if I hurt her? Tool is an ass. I do not have a small cock, and now I know she's wondering if I do, just like he wanted. I know once I drop my pants, the small bit of worry in her head will ease, but I want to kick Tool's ass for even making her think it.

Her face is hidden for a moment when I pull off her shirt. That long raven hair lays to the left across the mattress, reminding me of a pool of ink, so shiny, so dark. I forget how to breathe when I see her lying there in her bra, a simple black one that makes her skin look as pale as the moon. It's the bra

I got her. I'll never forget asking the sales associate for help looking for a bra. I was the only man in the store, but the way it pushes her tits up, I'll say I did a great fucking job.

I place another kiss on her lips, keeping it languid and gentle. Part of me wants to give her a chance to say no, to come to her senses, but the other part of me has to feel her. My fingers feel for the clasp and unsnap it. I push away, breaking the kiss, and slide the straps down her arms.

"Goddamn," I groan when the palm-sized tits finally show. She's pure perfection. She really was ripped from my imagination, a wet dream come to life. Her nipple is a dark red, the size of a quarter and tightened, begging for my mouth.

And that flush? It stops at her chest. I lean down and press my lips between the valley of her breasts, feeling the strong thump of her heart beating against the flesh of my mouth. She trusts me with this, trusting me to cherish it and take care of it. I will. I'll make her heart beat stronger every day with my effort to love her more, love her harder, until she fucking flies.

I cup her tits, and my head falls back on my shoulders as the soft tissue presses against my palms. I knead them, plucking the nipples and tugging them, bringing soft moans from Scarlett's lips.

Jesus Christ.

I want to record those noises and listen to them on repeat.

"Jenkins."

Fuck yes, I want to record that too, the sound of my name filled with lust and need. She fucking needs me, and that nearly makes me come in my jeans. I'm about to burst. I can't wait any longer. I fall forward and slam my lips against hers, touching her body with vigor, pawing at her like a damn dog. I unbutton her jeans, never breaking the kiss, and her arms wrap around my neck, pressing her lips harder against mine. She sucks my tongue into her mouth, and I swear to fucking god, it's a direct link to my cock.

I moan down her throat, my eyes rolling back to see the black nothing of my skull. I imagine her doing that to my cock, sucking me deeper into her mouth like a greedy little whore. I have to break the kiss to get her pants off, and the damn things are so tight, they're suctioned to her.

"What the fuck," I growl when the pants won't get past her thighs, which are thick and curvy, and all I want to do is sink my teeth into them.

She giggles, covering her mouth with her hands as she laughs at me.

"Oh, you think that's funny?" I taunt her. "You think it's funny to leave my cock hard and your pussy wet because your pants won't come off?"

"Mmmhmm," she hums, reaching for my chest and rubbing my pecs.

"Joke's on you, sugar." I reach into my back pocket and take out a knife that Tongue gave me a few years ago. I don't use it much, so I know it is sharp, and it's going to cut right through those damn pants. She's never allowed to wear shit like that again. If it isn't accessible for my hands and my cock, then she can't wear it. "You trust me?"

Her throat moves as she gulps. Her chin touches her chest in a slow nod, and her big blue eyes are so wide that I see the whites of her eyes. The sharp metal gleams against her pupils, and that demonic part of me shakes with how beautifully fucked up it looks.

I make a mental note to make sure I lavish her neck with kisses and maybe leave a few marks. Show her off a bit when I take her out and when guys see my mark on her, they'll know to back the fuck off.

Pinching the waistband of her pants, I press the blade against it, one side against her skin, the sharp side against the constricting, illegal pants that I never want to see again. The rip of denim ripping sounds, and when I've cut enough of it, I throw the knife somewhere off to the side and grab the jeans with my hands, then yank.

They tear all the way down to the ankle, and her legs are longer than I thought. I can't wait to have them wrapped around my hips as I pound into her, her heels digging into my ass with every quick curl of my hips.

Now all that's left on her are cotton panties and they're wet, showing the curves of her lips. "You're a goddamn vision, sugar. I bet that pussy is going to taste so sweet, I'll be addicted and never be able to get enough."

"I hope not." Her hands fall to her sides and grip the sheets when my fingers curl into the thin band and yank, shredding them until they're tattered pieces of cloth in my hands. I lean between her legs, hug her hips with my arms, and pull her down on my face, burying my nose into the slit of her pussy.

"Oh fuck, you smell so good." I rub my nose between her folds, and her bare cunt rubs against my face. My sugar must have shaved for me.

"Jenkins, please. I need you."

I need her too, so damn much; it's a visceral need that I depend on to keep me sane. I don't wait any longer, I spread her lips and flatten my tongue, licking from the back to feel her puckered star, to the front where her clit rolls beneath me. I moan, sucking the sweet piece of candy into my mouth and nibbling on it. She arches her back and wraps her arms around my back, digging her sharp nails into my skin. I feel my flesh give and break, and my cock punches against my zipper, loving the slight pain.

I reach down and unzip my pants and push them off, then realize I forgot to take off my boots. "Fuck. Hold on, I need to take off my boots, sugar."

"No! Just get inside me, please." Scarlett sounds like she's on the verge of tears.

I fall forward and brace my arms on either side of her body and settle between her legs. "You sure? No going back, sugar. You're mine."

"I never want to be anyone else's."

I want to believe her, but I don't know if it's lust talking or truth.

I'm going with truth because it's my own.

"Wait." She pushes me off her, and for second, I worry I hurt her. She eyes my cock and smiles, plopping down on the bed. "Thank god. You're huge. I was scared."

"I'm going to kill Tool," I say through tight teeth, feeling the need to beat the living shit out of him.

"Don't think of him. Think of me." She grabs the back of my neck and pulls me in for another kiss. I settle between her legs again, feeling those long limbs wrap around me, and it feels just as good as I thought. We're anchored together, and in one hard thrust, I sink into her, lodging my cock in her awaiting depths.

"Jenkins!" she yells, and her pussy clamps around me already. My eyes cross from the immense pressure of the tightness massaging me, and her body shakes from her quick orgasm. "Oh my god," Scarlett moans, plucking her nipples with her fingers as she licks her lips. "Yes, Jenkins, you feel so good. Make me come again. Just the feel of you inside me set me off. I want more. Give me more."

She sounds like a fucking porn star, and Scarlett rubs her hips against me impatiently, fucking herself on my cock.

"Jesus, that's it. Ride my cock, sugar. Use me," I urge her, straightening my spine to watch my cock slide in and out of her tight heat. Fucking hell, my cock is soaked from the drag of her pink lips sucking me.

I'm not going to be able to last much longer. It's been too long, and she feels too fucking good. Her ass is off the bed, her back against the mattress, and she tosses her head left and right as she takes her pleasure, as she claims what is hers.

Me.

"Oh fuck," she shouts. "Yes, Jenkins. Yes! Your cock is so fucking good." She grits her teeth as she slams her pussy down on me harder, my heavy cum-swollen sack slapping against her ass. She has a filthy mouth in bed. I fucking love it. "You're going to make me come." She purses her lips on a moan, and my spin tingles, swirling my lower belly with my orgasm. "Jenkins! Jenkins!" She lifts her hips off me and thrusts down on me one more time. "Best fucking dick ever. Yes, Jenkins."

That's it. We're making videos so I can relive every time we fuck because she's too hot, and I need a reminder of how the hell I have a woman as fiery as her beneath me right now.

My cock is suddenly drenched, my balls dripping with her nectar. She used me, and now I'm going to use her. I yank my cock out of her, flip her over, and stare at her round ass for a second. My cock is pointing straight to her entrance, and I want nothing more than to bury my face in her and eat her puckered hole as I scissor fuck that tight cunt.

But I need to come, and her pussy feels too good to wait much longer. I slap her ass, and she yelps, but it's followed by a high-pitched whine as she waves her ass in the air to get another slap. Her skin is already pinking up from the first one, and my cock leaks come from the sight.

Not pre-cum.

White drops of fucking cum because she has me so close to the edge.

I press my hand against her shoulder blades to hold her down and slide home in one stroke. "Fucking hell, never in my life has as pussy felt so good, sugar. I'm going to fuck you every day."

"I'm going to be the only pussy you ever fuck, Jenkins," she snarls, angry like a jealous girlfriend, and something about that rubs me the right way.

I slap her ass again and slide my hand up her side until I grip her hair, using it like reins as I fuck her hard, relentless, and ruthless.

"You're going to take every drop, aren't you, sugar? Every drop of my cum? You're going to drink me up because your cunt is so thirsty for me."

"Yes," she says at the same time as she clutches the sheets in her hand, trying to hold onto something to keep her steady.

I'm grunting, sounding like a feral beast as I hammer inside her sweet body. Our skin slaps, and her moans are loud. No way no one can hear us. The walls are thin, and that makes me fuck her harder, cranking up her noise level just a tad.

"Jenkins, I'm-I'm—"

"Do it! Come all over me again." Because I'm about to

shoot my seed so far inside her, she's going to be seeping with my cum for days.

Her pussy spasms around me again, and I scratch my dull nails down her spine, slick with sweat. "Scarlett!" I thrust in deep. "Sugar, oh, fuck!" I moan each word as my fucking soul leaves my body while hot jets of come leave me, my orgasm nearly changing the reality I see around me.

With every rope that speeds from me, my hips spasm to get my cock in deeper, doing what my natural instincts want me to do.

Fuck.

Claim.

Breed.

CHAPTER SEVENTEEN

Scarlett

"**C**OME ON, SUGAR. WAKE UP. I NEED TO INTRODUCE YOU to everyone," Boomer croons at me as his fingers run through the tangles of my hair.

"No," I grumble, flipping over in the opposite direction. I'm not a morning person. I'm not really an afternoon person either. It takes me five hours to really wake up and get on with my day. "Go 'way," I slur with sleep, wanting to get back to my dream.

"Sorry, sugar. I can't do that. We need to meet with the guys. Your friends will be there, along with Homer."

I grab the pillow and throw it at him, then roll to the other side of the bed and get up. My body is aching everywhere, and that's when I remember all of our rounds of sex last night. Muscles I had no idea could be sore are sore, and my pussy, my god … the bone even hurts. Is it possible to bruise bone during sex?

BOOMER

"Feeling alright, sugar?"

"Better than ever," I say with a yawn, stretching my arms above my head. Boomer's eyes fall to my bare breasts and fill with heat.

"You're going to be trouble with a capital fucking T." He adjusts his erection, and something he said last night comes back to me. He said he hadn't been able to get an erection before. I wonder why...

"Hey, Boomer? Can you talk to me about everything? About you?"

He scratches the side of his head, something he does when something is swirling inside that mind, but I have no idea what it is. I want to be let in. "Yes, just not today."

"When?"

"I don't know," he says as he hangs his head, gripping the dresser with his hands. "I'm afraid to tell you. Just know I'm a little screwed up in the head, and if that's too much for you—"

I lay my hand on his shoulder and kiss the ink there, the flames of a burning home. "I meant what I said. I want to get to know you. I want to know everything. Nothing you say will change that."

"I'm not ready to talk about it with anyone." He turns away from me and snatches a shirt from the drawer.

"Okay, I won't push it. I'm sorry."

"No." He exhales and pulls me to him. I smell fresh soap and a hint of leather against him. It smells so good. Where the leather is coming from is confusing me. Maybe it's cologne. Whatever it is, I love it. "I'm sorry. Listen, I'm not a great man. I'll do my best to be what you need, but—"

My heart sinks when I hear the dreaded word.

"I'll never be good enough for you, but I don't want to ever let you go."

I love it when he holds my jaw like I'm something fragile that can be broken. "You're my boom," I whisper, wishing he'd tell me more, but I know if he never did, I'd be okay with it. I'll love him regardless because I see more of him than he could ever see.

He might think he's fucked up, but he's my kind of fucked up, my mess, and I want him just the way he is—a little crazy and a whole lot of passionate.

"Scarlett, I'm not Prince Fucking Charming. I'm not a savior. I'm someone's worst nightmare, and you're about to find out things about me when you meet my friends, my family, that you might not ever look past—"

I silence him with my finger and shake my head. "You forget that you're my Prince Charming. You did save me. Sure, you might not look the part, but you fit it just as good, if not better."

His forehead falls to mine, and a gust of wind rustles the curtains beside us, breezing over our skin. It's a cooler day, and it reminds me that I'm still naked and need to get dressed, but Boomer's fingers dig into the flesh above my ass. "I'm halfway in love with you, sugar. You can't go saying shit like that."

"I can if I'm halfway in love with you too."

He smashes his lips against mine, and a quick taste of his tongue makes me whimper. "Get dressed or we'll never leave this room."

"Is that so bad?" I tease him, rubbing my finger down the deep divot of his pecs.

"No, but if we don't go out there now, I'll get my ass whooped, and I'm really debating if it will be worth it because you look so fucking hot naked right now. Go." He slaps my ass, and I yelp, running away from him, a loud laugh falling from my lips.

I grab a sundress off a hanger and slip it over my head. It's simple. A flowy black skater-dress. It falls a little lower than my mid-thigh and since my breasts are small, a bra isn't needed. I throw my hair up in a messy bun and brush my teeth. "K, I'm ready!"

"I didn't see you put on panties." He lifts a brow at me, licking his lush lips.

I sashay my hips as I walk toward him. "Because I didn't."

A loud, frustrated groan leaves him, and he pushes the dresser he put against the door last night out of the way, and the door immediately falls to the ground. "Let's go, sugar. You're about to drive me fucking nuts, which says something."

When I'm outside, I notice the gray skies and how they're rolling above the water, sucking in that moisture to prepare for rain. Another gust of wind comes, and it blows up my dress. Boomer's hands land on my ass, gripping the cheeks, and I fall back against him, rubbing my bare rear over his hard cock.

"Anyone could see this, you know."

"Isn't it fun?"

He spins me around, picks me up, and slams me against the motel wall. "Let me tell you something—you're mine. No one else can see you, any part of you, and if you want to show your ass, you're only going to show it to me. And then I'm going to fuck you to show you that you're mine."

"I already know I am. I just like to tease you."

He puts me down, and my pussy slides against his cock. It hits my clit just right, and I whimper, wishing he'd slid into me right here. I'll have to warm him up to the idea of someone watching us one day. I think he'll love it.

"Boomer! Let's go!" a man shouts at him from the hallway.

"I have a feeling you're going to get me yelled at all the time," Boomer mutters, taking my hand and dragging me behind him as we walk down the dark hallway.

The dark.

I really hate the dark.

I tighten my hand around his and do my best to be brave, but all I see are the chains and I can smell urine and stagnant water. I hear boots. So many boots thudding above me.

"Scarlett, hey, I got you, sugar. I got you." Boomer spins around suddenly and picks me up. I wrap my legs around him and lay my cheek against his shoulder. Safe. I'm safe as long as I am in his arms. "I got you. Nothing is going to happen to you," Boomer says and even though the hallway is dark, his voice brings light, and I'm able to take a breath again.

We walk through a door, and the room is quickly illuminated. It smells like moth balls and old man, which makes sense, since it's the office that Homer stays in most of the time. The guys are seated in various chairs, some standing, and the girls are sitting on the floor. Boomer puts me down, and I run over to Melissa who looks scared out of her mind.

The guys cheer and slap Boomer on the arm, and I'm confused as to why.

"Jenkins! Jenkins. Oh, you fuck me so good, Jenkins!" the man mocks as he slugs Boomer on the arm.

"Oh god." I hide my face in my hands when I realize they heard me last night.

"Looks like you don't have a little dick after all; not after all that howling we heard!" some guy that I don't know slaps his knee, tossing his head back. For some reason, I feel the need to defend Boomer.

I stand and point my finger at the man with a screwdriver nestled above his ear. "His cock is huge, and I'm still sore. So all of you can shut up and stop giving him a hard time and get on with this meeting."

Another guy with poofy hair and a young look about him squeals. "A hard time..."

All the guys snicker, and Boomer smacks the guy on the back of the head. "Poodle, shut up."

"Why am I always the one getting slapped in the head!"

"'Cause you're a fucking idiot." The man who just spoke is huge with tattoos down his arms, and they peek under the collar of his shirt. He's older and exudes power and authority. I can't help but to sit down and listen. "Alright, we have a lot to talk about, and it all starts with you ladies."

All eyes fall on us, and Melissa grips my hand. I clutch her fingers tight because while they are different than the men who took us, these men are also very similar.

I've gone down one rabbit hole only to come out and fall down another.

"Now, in order to make you ladies more comfortable, everyone is going to go around and introduce themselves. You're safe here, okay?"

I nod, believing the man in charge. Homer walks in at that moment, carrying a tray that has a large pitcher of tea and some plastic cups. "Here you guys go."

"Thanks, Homer," Boomer says.

"Anytime." His old voice shakes. He plops down in a ripped leather chair that looks just as old as he is.

"Alright, I'm Reaper. I'm Boomer's stepdad."

I want to ask what they do because their names are similar to the bikers who took us. Boomer would have told me, right?

"I'm Tool." He half-ass waves and sticks a screwdriver behind his ear.

"I'm Poodle." He waves happily, his hand going a hundred
miles an hour.

"Poodle?" Melissa asks softly. "Cause of your hair?"

Tool snickers. "Told you, you had bitch hair; just like your
dog."

"Fuck you! My dog is elegant and fucking classy."

Melissa giggles, and it's the first time I've ever heard it.
Poodle's head turns to Melissa, and his cheeks blush. He's
adorable.

"I'm Knives." He's handsome, but cleaner cut than the others. His hair is short, and he doesn't have tattoos.

"You know me. I'm Badge." He has tattoos everywhere.
His shaved head and cold eyes give him a look that tells me not
to fuck with him.

No worries there.

"I'm Tongue," a voice says from ... somewhere. "You
know me."

All the girls turn around and look to see who's speaking,
but they can't find a soul.

"Tongue, come out from the fucking corner," Reaper says
with exhaustion. "You're being creepy. We've talked about this."

"I like corners," Tongue says slowly. "I see everything."

His voice sounds like the monster in horror movies.

"I'm Bullseye. It's 'cause I love darts, if you're wondering."
He is big, muscle on top of muscle.

"You could say that," Tool grumbles under his breath, and
Reaper hits him on the back of the head.

"Ha! Fuck you. That's what you get." Poodle sticks his
tongue out, and suddenly, Tongue steps out of the shadow and

grips it. Poodle yells, and all the guys laugh, but I don't find it funny.

"You need to be more careful what you do with that thing," Tongue scolds Poodle, whipping out his knife. "It's been so long." The man truly terrifies me. He saved Boomer, but the way he's rubbing his knife against Poodle's tongue... it's almost like he is hypnotized.

"Leave him alone!" Melissa speaks up, and all eyes turn to her. Her voice has no heat, but she gets up on shaky legs, using my shoulder to push herself up to stand straight. "You aren't being nice."

"I'm not nice," Tongue hisses, pushing Poodle away by his tongue.

"What the fuck, man?" Poodle sounds like he can't feel his tongue, mumbling the words.

"You shouldn't have stuck it out," Tool jabs.

"Children. Jesus. All of you. Get. Back. On. Track." Reaper claps his hands after every word, but Melissa stares Tongue down, unafraid still.

"The little one is creeping me out. She's staring at me," Tongue whispers louder than intended to Reaper as he shrinks back in the shadows, as if he never existed in the first place.

"This is getting out of hand," Reaper says, and Boomer rubs a hand over his mouth, hiding a smile as he winks at me. It tells me everything is going to be okay. Maybe all of this is normal.

"First..." Reaper grabs his chair and flips it around before sitting down. He has a silver wedding band on his finger, and I shouldn't be surprised that the man is married, but I am. All of them seem too rough to know how to love, but then I look at Boomer, and I know I'm wrong.

Everyone is capable of love.

"I need to know what happened to each of you and how you got to the basement of that clubhouse. Second, I need to tell you that a few of us are going to make a trip over there for a visit."

I shake my head, and Melissa panics, shaking her head quickly as she hurries toward the door to escape, but Poodle grabs her, whispering something in her ear.

"I'm not going back there," I say.

"No, no," Reaper reassures. "You girls are staying here."

"How can you make a visit? You don't know them."

"I know enough," Reaper says. "This motel is now a safehouse. I've talk to Homer about it. He's alright with it. A few guys will stay behind and keep you safe. Me, Boomer, Tool, Bullseye, and Tongue, we're heading out tonight. Word has it they're having a party, and I want answers. Ladies, start from the beginning."

I'll ask Boomer why he has to go later. Joanna, Abigale, and Melissa keep their mouths shut, so I start my story first.

"And don't leave a single detail out," Reaper warns.

I go back to the first thing I remember.

Campus.

CHAPTER EIGHTEEN

Boomer

WOLF, KNIVES, AND BADGE TAKE THE GIRLS SHOPPING AND out to eat. I gave Scarlett my debit card and told her to have a grand time. I have plenty of money for only being twenty, but that's what happens when your dad leaves a shit-ton of money after he dies, and every dime I made after that just added to it.

The girls can't be around because we're loading up to pay a visit to the Atlantic City chapter. I think Scarlett is on to me, though. She knows something is off, and I'm hiding something. Lies never stay buried, and if I don't speak the truth soon, I'll get buried along the lie I've tried so hard to hide.

Everyone can lie. Reaper's words echo in the back of my mind.

"Are we killing tonight?" Tongue asks as he sharpens his blade. He never carries a gun, only blades. And his favorite stays strapped to his side.

"Not if we can help it," Reaper says, shrugging on his cut. It's been so long since I've seen it, and I immediately miss what I left behind.

I hold my cut in my hand, debating if I want to put it on; not because I don't want to, but because I know I don't deserve it.

"I wouldn't want you to put that on either." Tool decides to chime in as he loads his gun in the holster. "It's not like you deserve it."

"Tool!" Reaper slams his palm on the table. "We can't have shit like that between us tonight. We have no idea what we're about to see or do. We need to be prepared and have each other's backs. If you can't do that, then you can stay here. You're my VP, and you still owe a debt for what you did to my wife; this would only be the beginning. Don't act like you're fucking perfect," Reaper snarls. "Do I make myself clear?"

"Yes, Prez," Tool obliges and shrugs his cut on, glaring at me through hateful eyes.

It's going to take a long time for me to gain Tool's trust back. Staring at the same cut my father wore, I put it on, and something inside me eases. I had no idea how much I missed it. I've grown in the short amount of time I've been gone. I've realized things about myself that I would have never come to terms with back home in Vegas.

I'm ready.

"Good. Everyone ready?" Reaper asks, eying all of us. "Good. Let's ride."

Tool is out the door, stomping his heavy boots like a child having a tantrum. Reaper shakes his head in disappointment and tugs his hand through his hair. I'm not nervous. If anything, I'm excited. I have my lighter, grenades, dynamite;

everything a man needs to have a good time. I'm ready to blow shit up.

"I see that fucking look in your eye. Forget it. It isn't happening. Not tonight."

"I don't know what you're talking about, Reaper," I say with a shrug of my shoulder as I mount my bike. I haven't ridden in days. Why have I ignored this part of myself? Why have I hated it? It's who I am. I'm made for this.

Ruthless is in my blood, and I can't turn my back on it again. I fucked up once, and I refuse to repeat history.

Reaper snorts and revs the loud engine of his bike. "Yeah, I just bet you don't, kid."

I toss my head back in a sardonic laugh, rolling out of the parking lot and onto the road. Since I know where this shithole of a clubhouse is, the guys follow me. The bikes roar down the highway, the lights of the casinos painting the night sky, while the ocean rolls to the right. It's fucking beautiful here.

I wouldn't mind staying, but I don't know how that can happen. My home is far away from here, but going anywhere without Scarlett isn't an option. I can't hang my cut up again, not for anybody. That's not today or tomorrow, so I don't have to think about it now.

With the wind in my hair and the smell of the ocean in the breeze, another piece of me heals as my mind quiets. Only people who have constant turmoil in their heads will understand what I'm going through. It's an uphill battle, trudging through mud and self-judgment. I lose half the time, believing the things my mind tells me.

But I'm getting better.

Piece by broken piece of me, I'm becoming whole.

We drive fifteen minutes and roll down a road that I can

tell isn't used a lot. We get deeper into the woods, away from the noise of the boardwalk, a place I really want to take Scarlett when all this is over, but I can't have her in public with this hanging over her head.

The old wooden house comes into view on the right. Bikes are parked along the gravel path, and a few members are outside wearing their cuts and getting blown by their club whores. This place is bad. I knew that when I saw it the first time, but seeing it again with everyone here, I can't believe this chapter is still active.

There's a shack behind the house with chains, and I know whatever they have hiding back there can't be good.

The roof is sagging, and the shingles are peeling off. The house itself looks like it hasn't been lived in for centuries. The paint is worn, and the wood is rotted. It's a shame something so ugly is surrounded by a beautiful environment. The trees are tall and bright green, leaves galore creating shadows from their canopies, and this backwoods fucking MC has their junk littering all over it—old cars and parts and trash.

Out in the front yard there is a fire pit roaring, and a few guys have their shirts off, smoking weed from the smell of it, and staring at us like we're trespassers.

Please. If anyone is a trespasser, it's them; stepping all over the Ruthless King brand how they are. I want to unclip a grenade and shove it in their mouth just like I did Sarah's abuser. Just thinking about it has shivers of anticipation tremoring my skin. Fuck, I need something like that, and maybe I'll feel better.

The bikes loud, grumbling engines come to a stop as we park away from the club's motorcycles. I want my shit nowhere near them, just in case their scum rusts my fucking wheels.

"Damn, he looks like shit," Reaper says, staring at a man

who just walked out the front door to lean against the porch beam. He's a big guy, not bigger than Reaper, but almost. He doesn't have on a shirt, just his cut, and his hair flows down to his waist, greasy and unwashed. He smokes a cigarette as he looks our way.

"You know him?" I ask from the side of my mouth.

"Kid, I know all the fucking Prezs in the Ruthless chapters. I haven't seen Venom in a long time, though." We all slowly walk toward the clubhouse, and I can't believe my ears. Reaper knows these assholes. "And no, I had no idea what he was doing."

That answers my next question.

"Holy shit, if it isn't the man himself," Venom greets with a large smile. His teeth are yellow and rotted, and his arms are laced with track marks from drugs. Just what the hell is going on here? Venom prances down the steps happily, and his crew backs him as he meets Reaper halfway.

"Venom. It's always good to see you, man. Been a long time." Reaper hugs him, slapping him on the back like they're old time friends who used to kick back and have a beer.

He has some explaining to do.

Venom looks truly happy to see Reap. He smiles, keeping his hands on Reaper's arms, patting his biceps every few seconds. "Fuck, man, it's been what ... fifteen years? What the hell brings you to my neck of the woods? Come on inside. I'll have the prospects bring you and your crew some beer."

"Ah, my boys never got to throw me a bachelor party, so we came to the city, and let me tell you, it has not disappointed!" Reaper hoots, and Tool howls in pursuit, hyping the lie up as much as he can.

Venom grabs Reaper's left hand and looks at the wedding

band. "Holy fucking shit; you got married? The Reaper? The same guy who had different pussy every night in his bed for years. Shit, we have to celebrate." Venom throws his arm around Reaper's shoulders. "Atlantic City never disappoints! Does it, boys?" he asks his brothers, and all the guys holler and clap. "We're going to get fucked up tonight and, Reap, my man, I have a few things in store for you. You're going to fucking love it."

Yeah, something tells me we're going to hate it, and we're leaving here tonight without doing a goddamn thing because we need them to think we're on their side before we take them down. We need more information. Are there more girls? Are other chapters involved in this? The girls who have been sold, can we save them?

So much information needed and not enough time to get it.

The place is familiar to me as we walk inside. I immediately look toward the basement door, the one that hides their secrets and torment. I want to go and see if there are women down there who need help, but I can't, and it kills a little part of me.

The clubhouse is a lot different than the one in Vegas. This one is a plain looking house, definitely not enough room for all the members to come and stay if they wanted. A few poker tables, plain round tables, and there's a makeshift stage in the back with a stripper pole. Jesus, that thing looks like it's about to fall over.

"Like poker, huh?" I ask, knowing I have the best poker face anyone has ever seen.

"It's how we make our money, boy." Venom drags out a chair from the table. It has dark stains on it, some light, and I don't even want to know what they are. Fucking nasty. Don't get me wrong, men are fucking pigs, but this club, these people, they're dirty in every sense of what the word means.

"My name is Boomer, not boy," I growl in annoyance from the childish insult he just threw at me. Only Reaper and the men in *our* club get to call me whatever the hell they want. I sit and look around, seeing one of the rooms blown to bits from my grenade. "What happened there?" I tilt my chin to the scraps of wood that are broken and burnt. The dirt under the house shows, seeing a huge hole in the ground.

He holds up his hands. "Sorry, meant no offense. You're just young. You look like your balls have barely dropped."

I grind my teeth together, wanting nothing more than to kill the man. Maybe I'd play with him first. I'd make fuses out of his fingers, light them, and watch them spark. Yeah, that sounds good. I'll do that when I get the chance.

Reaper clears his throat, bringing the conversation back around. "Someone blew your place up. For what?"

One of their club whores walks from the bar, carrying a tray with a bottle of Jack and beer. As she comes closer, I notice a blue scarf around her neck, tied to the side. It's loose, and I can see the same mark Scarlett has on her neck. This isn't a club slut; this is a victim. Her eyes are a bit glazed over, her movements robotic and empty of all human motion. She's topless, tits out with bite marks on them, and her shorts should be considered panties with how much of her ass shows.

"They took some merchandise of mine, but you know what I think? I think it was one of my own. Hey!" He snaps his fingers like he has an idea, and he falls forward, the front two legs of the chair hitting the floor so hard, I swear one of the boards cracks. Hell, I'm not going to die in a fight; I'm going to fucking croak because the floor is going to fall out from under me, burying me in wood and nails. "You know what, you can help me find my property."

The woman places our drinks on the table, not looking at any of us, but I see the bruises over her body. The way Reaper stares at her and how he pops his neck tells me he isn't happy about what he sees too.

Another woman fumbles onto the stage, crying when she catches herself on her hands and knees. I'm sure the wood digging into her skin doesn't feel too good. I get up to help her, but Reaper tugs me back down by my cut, giving me a slight shake of his head.

"Stupid clumsy bitch." Venom throws a full beer bottle on stage, and it crashes right above the woman's head. She covers herself, screaming, and it's clear she's shaking. "Dance, whore!" he shouts, and Reaper laughs right along with him. Tool whistles by placing his fingers in his mouth, and Tongue isn't paying attention. He's carving a knife into the table with his knife.

The man is obsessed.

"What kind of merchandise are we talking about here, Venom?" Reaper takes a swig of his beer and makes a sound of delight when he swallows. "Fuck, that tastes good."

Venom crooks his finger as he leans his forearms on the table, telling us to come closer. "You know how the MC is. It's a business."

Reaper nods. "Yeah, I understand."

"Well, my business brings in good money. Women, Reaper. I sell women. Now, I know it's a little different, but the money is too good. Virgins sell for the highest, but we never get them because once I have 'em, I need that cherry for myself; you know what I mean?" Venom nudges Reaper in the side and takes a joint from his cut pocket. He places it in between his lips and inhales, sending a cloud of thick smoke in the air.

Tool chugs his beer, and Tongue is really shaving away at the table. The guys are getting pissed. Acting is exhausting when we agree with nothing Venom is talking about. How much longer is this going to go on for?

"One of my men, Wolf, took off the other day with four of my girls. There was one..." he says with a hungry grin and a lick of his lips. "She had long black hair and these small tits that were to die for."

I dig my fingers into my thighs and try to breathe, trying not to give me and the guys away by breaking character, but rage is blinding me. He's talking about Scarlett. My Scarlett. Mine. I can't be in here much longer. I'm going to kill him.

Kill them. Kill them. Kill them.

This time, I don't completely disagree with my intrusive thoughts.

I welcome them.

CHAPTER NINETEEN

Scarlett

T HE GRAINS OF SAND RUB AGAINST MY TOES AS I SIT ON THE beach, burrowing them as far as I can. I love the way the sand feels, gritty and rough, yet beautiful and soft all at the same time. I'm sitting on a soft blanket I got at the mall, a small cooler next to me, and a beer in my hand as I watch the waves.

It really is beautiful here.

With all the bad that happened to me, you'd think the first thing I'd want to do is leave this city, but it feels right, or maybe it's Boomer who feels right. I always heard people make a home; a place is just an empty idea without love and happiness. There's no meaning or importance to it if the heart isn't involved.

Well, mine is involved, and Boomer has become my home. I know wherever we go, every place will feel like that because he's with me.

I smile, thinking about last night, and bring the cold bottle to my neck to cool me down.

"And just what do you think you're doing out here all by yourself, sugar?"

"Boomer!" I squeal in excitement and get to my feet as fast as possible. I run over to him with a big smile on my face and jump toward him. He catches me in his arms and swings me off the ground as if he's just as excited to see me as I am him.

I toss my head back and laugh as he spins us around, and he brings us to the blue blanket I've laid out on the ground. I straddle his lap, staring into the dark eyes I've come to love.

"I fucking missed you, sugar."

I look down, nowhere particular, just the space between us, and grin. "I missed you too. How…" I hate to think about what it was like at the clubhouse. "How was it over there?"

He blows out a breath and lays back. His shirt rises, showing the skin above the waistband of his jeans. The dark happy trail makes my mouth water. I know exactly what that path leads to, and I want to follow it until my mouth is full, and my man is happy and sated.

"Kiss me first. I need to feel you."

I lower myself, my elbow bending to allow me to get closer. I keep my hair back with my other hand and place a soft kiss on the lips that changed my life.

"Nothing feels better than your lips. I needed that," Boomer says, rubbing his hands up and down my back. "Nothing feels better than you."

I fall to the side and prop myself up. "Are you okay?" My finger draws hearts on his chest, not that he will notice, but I know, and it gives me a small inkling of feeling like a little girl with a crush.

"I'm so lucky that Abigale came here. I know that's fucked up of me to say because she's still healing and when she got here, I thought she was going to die. If she didn't come here, I wouldn't have you. Those fucking animals would have you and—" he sits up and rubs his hands over his face. "I want to kill them, kill them, kill them," he says, slowly chanting in a sardonic tone. He sounds hypnotized. Maybe he has said this before? Or thought it? He sounds comfortable saying it, which I shouldn't be okay with, but I am. I hate those men and I want them dead. I wish I could kill them myself, but I don't have it in me.

I'm not a killer.

But Boomer is.

And I'm thankful he's relentless when it comes to me because the man in my corner will protect me until in the end.

"We have to go back. There are a few girls there walking around with the same marks that you and your friends have. They have a shed in the back, chained and locked. I need to know more. They want us to find the people who came in and took you ladies. They want us to be part of it, as a paid gig."

I scoot away and try to remain calm. He reaches for my hand. "I always need to be touching you. You quiet the chaos inside me."

"You do the same for me, Boomer. I need you to stay safe." I tickle the small stump where a finger used to be and hold his hand up to get a better look. "What happened?"

"I was beaten, strung up, and some fucker cut my damn finger off."

I blink at him, stunned, bothered, scared, curious, and so many other feelings and thoughts drift through me from his blunt statement. "Wha—Boomer, I need you to be safe. Is it those guys? Do they get you in trouble?"

"No, sugar. It isn't anything like that. I promise; I'll be alright." Boomer runs his fingers through the ends of my hair before pushing each side over my shoulders.

"Promise?" I ask quietly, wringing his shirt together between my fingers. "I'm nervous about this, Boomer. They aren't good men."

He shakes his head and cups my cheek, his thumb laying against the apples of my cheek, rubbing the pad of his finger side to side. "They aren't good men, but we are, and we have to put a stop to it, so it doesn't happen to other women, like you. God, how that Prez talked about you—"

"He talked about me!" I yelp and try to scatter off Boomer's lap, but his grip is strong and unwavering.

"Sugar, listen to me. I don't want to ever lie to you, but you are his first order of business."

Fear wraps around my throat, reminding me of that damn collar, and squeezes tight. Fear's fingers drip with blood and the broken dreams of others, but its hold isn't slippery. It's sure. It holdfast. It loves to take prisoners.

And I'm next.

"Sugar." Boomer tries his best to get my attention, but the beautiful beach morphs from the soft sand to the dark basement of the house, the water fades to chains, and the stars twinkling above are now the shadows of loud footsteps above me. I'm suddenly on my back, and Boomer is wiping away my tears. "Hey, look at me," he says sweetly.

I don't want to open my eyes because I'm afraid to see him. What if Boomer changes too? What if when I look at him, I see the men who chained me, hit me, tortured me?

"Look at me," he repeats, and this time I can't disobey him. I snap my eyes open, preparing to see someone else, but

Boomer's hazel eyes flicker that golden hue that I love, and his plump lips come closer to mine. Those lips can never be replaced by anyone else, they can never change; they're too unique, to precise in their skill. "There's my sugar," he says with a smile. "I'm never going to let anything happen to you. Ever."

I hold onto him tight. I scramble against him, lifting his shirt to feel his skin. Boomer is warm, and the shivers of that dreaded fear finally dissipates now that I have my hands on him.

"I love it when you touch me; you quiet all the noise." Boomer rolls his forehead against mine, breathing heavily. "You have no idea how loud it gets."

"What gets loud, Boomer? You can talk to me." I skim my hands up his shirt until my palms are on his chest. He gets more comfortable and settles between my legs. Boomer starts to kiss down my neck, and his hands grip my tank top, pulling it up and over my head then laying it beside me on the blanket. "Boomer." I try to get his attention, but he's igniting the fire inside me, slowly making me forget what we were talking about.

He works his way down one side of my body, then he kisses his way up the other. He sucks my earlobe into his mouth, and the sensual flick of his tongue lulls my hips to rock against his hard cock. "My head, sugar. You quiet all the fucked-up noise inside my head. You make me feel normal, feel human, and you have no idea how wonderful it is to finally feel peace." Boomer kisses my cheek. "You have no idea by just having that, I'm addicted to you."

"What goes on inside your head?" I ask, trying to keep some sense about me. Trying to speak right now is impossible. The air is humid with our lust, and I can hardly think of anything else when his body is on top of mine.

"Right now? Feeling that tight pussy around my cock," he

says with a wicked grin, nudging my lips open with his mouth. "You want that? Right here? Right now?" He grinds himself in the space of my legs, hitting my clit with every stroke.

"You said…" I swallow, coating my parched throat. "You said you didn't want anyone to see me—"

"They aren't." He slides his fingers under my shorts and dips inside my panties. "I'd never let anyone see my woman naked and bared to me. Your body is for me and no one else, Scarlett." Boomer pushes two fingers inside me, circling them around and around just like he does his cock. "So wet for me, sugar." He pulls out of me, leaving me needy and on edge. He brings his fingers up to his lips and sucks them into his mouth. Boomer's eyes roll back from my taste. "So fucking sweet, like nectar. Taste yourself."

I open my mouth, expecting him to put his fingers between my lips, but he shoves them between my legs unexpectedly. Just as I'm about to cry out, he removes them and silences me with his fingers. "Suck," he demands.

I wrap my tongue around his fingers and moan. I never thought I'd like how I taste. It's erotic and dirty.

The sound of his zipper is barely heard over the waves. They crash against the shore like my heart is against my rib-cage. He yanks his fingers free and reaches down to guide his cock between my legs. "Boomer—"

He slams his palm over my mouth and slides his long shaft to the hilt. His mouth drops open as he inches himself closer, our bodies still clothed, and the delicious rub of his jeans against my sensitive folds makes me groan, but it can't be heard, not when he's muting me with his large palm.

"I said to call me Jenkins. Anytime I'm inside this body, you'll call me Jenkins." He rears back and slams inside me.

"This is going to be fast, sugar. I want you too fucking much." Boomer dips his head to my shoulder and continues to pound into me and the drag of my shorts tickle my clit along with every punch of his cock.

Sand flies onto the blanket, and I dig my feet into the sand to stop us from moving, but every stroke he gives me is harder than the last, and it makes the blanket drag. I don't even care if I'm buried in the damn sand if it means experiencing this amount of pleasure.

Even with the cool breeze, my skin is sticky from the salt and sweat. My body gets hotter, my orgasm climbing to the stars, and I clutch onto Boomer, wishing he could be closer. I need him more. He must feel my desperate cling because he takes his hand off my mouth, replacing it with his lips. I pour my cries of pleasure down his throat, and he grunts in return. Stealing my hands in a hard grip, he slams them above my head and into the sand. They get buried from the pressure he puts on them, and he's able to get more leverage to curl his hips harder.

I rip my lips away and suck in a much-needed breath. "Jenkins!"

"Shhh, sugar. You're going to let everyone know what we're doing."

"Is that so bad?" I moan. "Jenkins, I'm so close. I'm right there."

"Yes, it's bad, and the fact you want people to see us makes me wonder if I need to fuck you harder to remind you who you belong to."

Belong.

"You're mine," he snarls, plummeting his thickness until my inner walls ache and clamp around him. "Now, fucking come before I have to kill someone for seeing you shatter beneath me."

If I were more stubborn, I wouldn't just to spite him, but the pleasure he gives me is out of this world, and my body let's go, obeying its master. I fall apart under him just like he wants, and a strong rumble of the orgasmic earthquake rumbling my core breaks me, sinking me deeper into the abyss of sand. My body is weightless, and now the only stars I see are the ones of blinding pleasure.

"Scarlett." My name is a light tremble in his throat as he comes, filling me up with his warm seed. He gives me a lazy kiss, timid and slow. We groan in unison when he pulls out of me, and his cum gushes out of me in a hurry; that's when I realize I have nothing to clean up with.

Boomer sees his fleeting cream and gathers it in his fingers to push it back inside me, and then he slides my panties into place to hold it. "I want you to walk around with me between your legs and maybe you'll remember the only man who needs to see you is me."

Like I could ever forget.

CHAPTER TWENTY

Boomer

"DO YOU REALLY NEED TO GO BACK TO THAT PLACE?"
Scarlett sits cross-legged on the bed, wearing my
t-shirt and little pink sleep shorts that make me wish
I didn't have to go back to that shithole.

"You know I do," I say, slinging the bag that contains my
cut and weapons over my shoulder. I've been lying to her all this
time. If I don't come clean soon, she's going to hate me, and it
will be the biggest regret I've ever had in my life. I'm too afraid
to tell her. I don't want her to think I'm like them, and I know
once she sees the cut, she'll run for her life.

I should chase her, but why would I when I know she'd be
better off without me?

"I know. I just… there's this weight on my chest when I
know you're there, and I can't breathe, Boomer. I can't breathe
knowing you're there and I'm here, because I just keep thinking—what if I never see you again?"

"Sugar, the only way you'd never see me again is if

I'm six-feet under." That's not the right choice of words because the heated rage in those narrowing blue eyes of hers makes me regret what I said instantly.

"This isn't a joke! They could kill you."

I drop the bag off my shoulder and sling it to the side. I don't give her time to get away. I cup her face and straddle her thighs, using my weight to keep her pinned down. She jerks her face away from me when I try to hold her chin, and a tear breaks free. "I'm sorry, sugar. Last thing I ever wanted to do was make you upset. You need to have faith in me. I love you, sugar. I need your faith, okay?"

"Oh, Boomer, you have my faith." Her cold palms grip my wrist that holds her delicate face. "It's them I'm worried about. They are ... they are..."

The word she's looking for is *ruthless.*

And she has no idea just how ruthless I can be too.

"Don't worry about me. I'll be back before you know it, and I want that hot little mouth wrapped around my cock."

Oh, that got her to stop being difficult.

"Hey, put your cock in your pants. We're heading out!" Tool bangs his fist against the new door Homer replaced earlier today.

"I got to go, sugar."

"No," she whispers, leaning her cheek against my hand.

I bring her lips to mine and kiss her like it's the last time. It won't be, but kissing like it's the last time? It's the best fucking kiss there is, so why not do it every time I walk out the door? "Fuck, you taste good. Alright, I need to go." Or I'll let the guys handle it and stay wrapped up in these sheets with my woman all day. Once all this is over, that's exactly what I'm doing. I'm going to lay her down on silk fucking sheets, so I can see that pale skin slide across something just as soft.

And then I'm going to dirty her up and ruin those fucking sheets with sweat stains and cum. Fuck, I'm getting hard thinking about it.

"Let's fucking go. Jesus, wipe the pussy juice off your face and get your ass in gear, Jenkins!" Tool bellows, nearly busting in the door again from the hard force of his fist. The fucker won't call me Boomer.

"Wait for me, okay?" I tell her, snatching the bag off the floor as I head to the door.

"I'll always wait for you, Boomer," she says.

I almost stop again, but I trudge ahead and open the door, leaving the only woman I've ever loved. I never thought it would be so damn difficult. Hearing her say she'll wait for me, damn it to hell; I'm a lucky man.

Women don't wait for guys like me.

I'm nowhere near perfect, but I'll do my damn best to be perfect for her.

I make my way out the door and jump off the porch, landing soundly in the sand. As I walk from the room to my bike, I think about all the things I want to do when this is over. I want to make things right with my family, with my sister, and apologize to her even though it will never be enough. Maybe I can go home and start my life again now that I've found what I was looking for to quiet my mind.

Scarlett.

"Jesus, thought I was going to have to tackle that big ogre again about coming to get you. He doesn't shut his damn trap, does he?" Homer bitches as he sweeps the walkway.

"Ha! You should tell him that, Homer. He'd love it."

"Maybe I will. I'm old, but I got a lot of fight left in me."

"I'll see you later, old man."

"Ah, fuck you, shithead," Homer grumbles, sweeping the dust and dirt at me. I try to get away from the cloud, laughing, but it sticks to my jeans anyway.

"'Bout fucking time. You think evil waits, Jenkins?" Tool says behind a cigarette as he lights it. "Typical. Fucking careless."

"Okay," I say, nodding. I toss my bag down and charge him. "You got something to say, Tool? Let's go. Fucking say it. I'm done with you. No more snide comments; say what you need to say."

Tool pushes against my chest, and I stumble, but not enough to lose my footing completely. I let out an angry cry, tackling the big fucker to the ground. I lift my fist back to slam it against his jaw. "You don't know fucking shit about me! You don't know anything!" I scream at him, and Reaper grabs my fist before I can throw another punch. "Let me go," I seethe.

"We don't have time for this shit. Get your head on straight and get on your bikes. You two can figure out your shit later, when there aren't abused women needing our help." Reaper pulls me off Tool in one tug, making me fly backward. Next, he grabs Tool by the cut and pulls him up too, his bicep flexing with the heavyweight. "I expect more from a seasoned VP. You're almost twice his age, Tool. He's young. He fucks up. He learns. Maybe you should do the same."

"Yes, Prez," Tool and I mumble at the same time. I don't give the VP another look. I go to my bike, mount it, start it, and fly out of there. The roar of the bikes follow behind me, and the adrenaline from fighting with Tool is coursing through my veins. I go faster, letting go of the throttle to gain more pavement in a shorter amount of time.

Ten minutes later, we're closing in on the clubhouse again, but we park down the road so they can't see us. This isn't about hanging out and shooting the shit; this is surveillance. Reaper and Bullseye are the only ones going inside.

I'm stuck with Tool. Luckily, I have the rest of the guys at my back, and I have a feeling Tool doesn't give a fuck about it. We push our bikes into the woods to hide them, and Reaper and Bullseye continue down the road, disappearing behind the cloud of dust.

"Know your way, boy scout?" Tool snips.

"Shut up, Tool. You know what Prez said. Just keep your mouth shut," Poodle says.

I appreciate Poodle more right now. I always thought he was just a big goof, but maybe there's more to Poodle than meets the eye. I slap him on the back and give him a tight smile. And good old Poodle, he gives me a happy-go-lucky grin.

Hunkering down, I push through the thin branches and wet leaves. A few briars catch my skin, pricking the surface enough for it to bleed. I watch my step, carefully placing my boots on clearer surfaces that don't have twigs or leaves. Our goal is to not make noise.

After a few minutes, we come to the tree line behind the shed that has my interest. I reach up and push a branch out of the way, shaking a bit of water down from the leaves onto my face. Reaper is outside still, talking to Venom. We have to wait for him to go inside. It's the only way. We left too early. The sun hasn't set yet.

"Shit," Tool hisses softly and hides behind a skinny tree. His shoulders show from either side.

A member of the club is walking behind the house, arm wrapped around a girl who's clearly strung out and unwilling. I lay down on the earth's floor, and Poodle, Badge, and Knives, follow suit. I'm hoping they go into the shed, but they don't.

The man stumbles and laughs, almost tripping over his drunken feet. Reaper sees the guy and points, laughing at him to show Venom that he's all in. Venom gestures the drunk asshole toward him, and they walk inside, the poor girl still attached to the man's arm.

Not for much longer. Not if I have anything to say about it.

Music blares from inside, and a few more bikes show up; not Ruthless Kings, but a different club. I can't see the backs of their cuts from here.

"What the fuck?"

For once, Tool says what I'm thinking. Surely other people aren't in on this.

I'm not sure how long we wait there, but it's dark, and the party inside is roaring. "Now's the time. Everyone ready?" Tool asks us.

"Yeah," I say. "And what makes you think that tiny tree can hide your fat ass?" I chuckle. What an idiot.

"I panicked, okay? Let's go." We inch from the woods like stealthy trained professionals. There's a glass breaking somewhere in the house, and it makes all of us freeze. "Jesus, I want to get out of here."

Me too. There are only a handful of us and an army of *them*.

"Hey, what's this?" Bullseye asks, stopping near a pair of doors that look like they go into the basement. The doors are old and rusted, yet another chain holds them down. Only certain people can get in, so no one can get out.

"It leads to the basement, where the girls were. I don't remember seeing another entrance, but I wasn't really focused on that. I wanted to get them out." I keep my voice as low as I can.

"I really want to kill these guys," Tool growls, taking out

his screwdriver and putting it in the lock. I'm not sure how he manages to unlock shit with one screwdriver, but he does, and I'm not going to question it.

I look over my shoulder to the shed, knowing this has to come first, but whatever is in there deserves our attention too. "We have to be quick."

"I know," Tool grunts as the lock pops free. "Bingo," he says happily. Slowly, he slides the chain free, so it doesn't clink loudly against the metal door. Tool looks around, making sure no one is around, and it makes the rest of us nervous, so we check too.

An owl hoots, and it causes me to jump.

Poodle chuckles, and I smack him on the back of the head. "Shut up."

"Still funny."

I mock him as I grab the rusted handle of one side of the door, and Tool grabs the other. We lift simultaneously, and it's much heavier than I expected. I plant my feet into the ground and huff out a strangled breath. Tool barely breaks a sweat.

The big fucker.

"Two of us go in. You guys be the lookout." Tool points to Badge, Knives, Tongue, and Poodle.

"You sure? You might need me," Tongue drawls, whipping is blade out. "I can be quick."

"You know what? Yeah, Tongue. Get down here," I tell him.

Tool hardens his eyes at me, and I lift my hands. "Better safe than sorry. I'd rather have his crazy ass down here than Poodle."

"That's not nice," Poodle mumbles.

"Sorry, Poodle. You aren't violent enough."

He nods in understanding and kicks the ground. "That's fair."

Jesus, never thought that would hurt someone's feelings.

"Okay, enough fucking pillow talk. We only have an hour to scope the place. Let's go." Tool heads into the darkness first, and Tongue follows, then me. Whimpers and cries echo through the basement. I'm reminded of Scarlett and her fear, and I want nothing more than to help these girls, but we can't today. We don't have the time or the resources. It's only about gathering information.

"I'm going to cut the tongues out of every member in the chapter for doing this." Tongue's voice rattles with bitterness and the promise of bringing hell down on the men that did this.

"Please, don't hurt us," one of the girls cries. She's bundled up in a corner in a tight ball, the same collar around her neck that Scarlett once wore. "Please."

"Darlin', no one is going to hurt you, okay? We're the good guys." Tool inches forward softly. "I know you see the cuts and the same name, but we're a different chapter. You don't know what that means, but we're safe."

"Are you going to get us out of here?" another woman says from the other side of the room.

"Not tonight. We're sorry." Tool doesn't beat around the bush, and it makes all the women sob uncontrollably, nearly sending me to my knees. We're their only hope, and we're letting them down.

"Don't leave us down here, please," another says.

God, how many are there? They keep speaking up. My head starts to swim with anxiety, and I clutch each side when the thoughts scream at me.

You're a failure. You're weak. You can't save them all. They're as good as dead, and you killed them.

"No, no, no." The words are small and distorted as they fall from my lips. No one hears me... except Tongue.

"Don't listen to it," Tongue whispers to me. "You're better than the enemy in your head; believe me."

I think I'm going crazy.

"Please," a woman's sad voice, still full of hope, calls out.

"We're gathering information on how to help you guys. Just a few more days, okay? I need you guys to hang in there." Tool looks just as hopeless as I feel as he looks at each woman. He knows they might not have a few days. "We will come back for you, okay? As fast as we can. We aren't prepared tonight."

"You swear?" the one who spoke first asks. "Because you have no idea what they're going to do to us in those two days." She turns away, disheartened, and a part of me wonders why we have to wait. Why not take them now?

Because they'll come to the motel, and we need more men. Reaper needs to call in the cavalry.

"We'll come back. I don't care if the effort kills me," Tool tells all of them. He turns his back, and all his brothers follow—me included—and it's the hardest fucking thing I've ever done. We climb the steps out of the basement, and every damn time my foot hits the ground, I feel like I'm doing the wrong thing by leaving these women to their own defenses. Poodle, Knives, and Badge are standing there, looking vigilant and at the ready.

"That bad?" Poodle asks.

With heavy hearts, Tool and I close the doors with a resounding clatter, trapping the girls inside once again. We slide the chain through the handles and lock it. "Worse," I say to the guys. "So much fucking worse."

Tool blows out a breath, staring at the closed doors that lead to hell, and I feel like the devil for having to walk away. A loud commotion from out front makes us pause, and then we look for a hiding place, but nothing is in view. "Behind the shed, go!" Tool hisses, and we all sprint behind the one damn place we came here to look in.

We place our backs against the wood, my chest heaving, but the small promise of having to light something on fire to protect us has me trembling with excitement.

"Reaper, this is what I have to show you," Venom slurs, and the familiar rattle of the chains sliding out of the doors let us know he's about to go inside the shed. "The ultimate paradise, Reap. You're going to love this."

The creak of the doors is loud even through the beat of the music from the house. "We made each stall a room. You know, for the men who want to have a little taste of their product before they buy."

"What are they doing up there?" Reaper's asks.

"Those are the fucking traitors who don't agree with me. Isn't that right, Kansas?"

I give Tool a questioning look before hearing a low moan of pain. It sounds like a man.

"That's Kansas, One-Eye—don't let the two eyes fool you; one is made of glass—and that's Arrow, my old VP. How's it hanging, Arrow?" Venom cackles. "They get to watch as I live out what I'm destined to do. Since they hate it so much. Don't have room for traitors, Reaper."

"Me either, Venom."

There's an underlying tone in each statement they said to one another. A silent threat.

Question is, who's going to make good on that threat?

CHAPTER TWENTY-ONE

Scarlett

BOOMER BARELY SPEAKS TO ME WHEN HE RETURNS FROM THE clubhouse. Whatever happened tonight really got to him. He looks defeated, and the battle hasn't even really begun. The shower turns on, and I debate if I want to go in there to comfort him. He doesn't seem like he wants company.

Too bad. I won't let him lock himself away in his mind. I'm here to help him, and he's going to have to get used to that. I take off my shirt and slip off my panties. When I get to the bathroom, I pull the shower curtain back and see him leaning against the tile, eyes shut, head hanging as the water sprays against his back.

I step inside and close the curtain and get on my knees, wanting to service him tonight. He deserves it. I run my hands down his slick body, and the ridges of his abs roll against my palm. His cock lays against his thigh, and the dark hairs on the white of his flesh are wet, sticking to him. It's beautiful.

Just like him.

"I don't know, Scarlett. I have a lot in my head tonight," he says, squeezing his eyes and turning his upper body away from me. "I want nothing more than your mouth on me, but—"

"No buts," I say, trailing my hands down the tree trunk of his thighs, so hard and defined. "I want you to let go. I'm here to cleanse your mind, Jenkins. Let go. Let me take care of you." I take his flaccid cock in my mouth and flick my tongue across the head. His hand flies to the back of my skull, and he groans, digging his blunt nails into my scalp.

"Fuck, you may be right, sugar. Your lips need to be wrapped around me more often." He tosses his head back into the rush of water.

He quickly firms up, and his nine-inch cock becomes too much to fit my lips around. I love looking at his dick. The plum-shaped head is a deep burgundy color from all the blood rushing to his girth, and I palm his heavy sack in one hand, loving how big they are just like the rest of him. I can't fit both in one hand. They're so full of his cum, and I want to release the pressure for him and make him feel at ease.

I lick the vein up the muscle and then back down before taking him in my mouth again. "You are so fucking good at blowing me, sugar. Yeah, just like that." One hand is flat against the tile behind me, and the other is still on my head as I bob up and down, slurping him as if he's a popsicle melting in the summer.

I need to make sure I get every inch before it's too late.

I roll his orbs in one hand, and he hisses. "Harder. Tug on them." I give a test tug, and he grunts. "More, fucking pull, sugar." The thin skin stretches as I tug and give a twist, hoping I don't hurt him. "Fuck!" He slams his fist against the wall. "Yes, just like that. Oh, fuck me," he groans.

I smile around the mouthful, feeling more confident than ever. I quicken my pace and flicker my eyes up at him through wet lashes. Water has soaked his hair, causing it to lay over his forehead and drip down on me like a waterfall. His eyes are almost black as he watches me.

He's a wicked want, a sinister promise.

And I plan to give in to both.

His defined body is sculpted with muscle and decorated in a few scars that I want to ask about. He hasn't had an easy life, one he doesn't really talk to me about, and I want to know it all. Why won't he give it to me. It angers me, and it makes me suck his cock with more vengeance. I'm here for him; why doesn't he know that?

I tighten my lips and take him to the back of my throat, giving him a tease of teeth along the way.

"I'm going to come!" He thrusts into my mouth until I gag, and I squeeze his balls tighter for making me do that, but I love it all at the same time. He holds my head down until my nose is buried in his thick dirty blond bush. "Oh, fuck," he moans, pumping me full of the salty goodness. It slides down my throat as I swallow greedily, loving the taste of him.

He slides out of me, still hard and aching. My clit is throbbing, and my hole is spasming for him to fill me up. I slide my hand down between my legs to ease the pressure, and he picks me up and flips me around. "Did sucking my cock turn you on, sugar? Does my dick in your mouth get you needy for me?" The words sound bitter, laced with poison as he rocks his cock between my cheeks.

"Please, Jenkins, please," I beg, hoping he makes me feel just as good.

Without warning, he plunges into me, and the unexpected force makes me cry out. Our wet skin slaps as he fucks me hard and fast, without gentleness, without care, just pure anger. "This pussy is so good. It's mine, isn't it. All fucking mine. No one else's. Not them. Not them. Not. Fucking. Them. Mine! Son of a fucking bitch; you're mine." He falls against my back, pumping his cock in and out of me as he kisses the back of my neck. "Tell me, sugar." I've never heard him sound so desperate before.

I push him back with my ass and flip around, wrap my legs around his waist, and circle my arms around his neck. "Yours, Jenkins." I lay my hand on his heart, and he slides in and out and hits all the right spots, deliciously sending all of my body into a frenzy of fireworks.

Kissing him, breathing him in, feeling the amount of turmoil he's giving me, I take it from him. I soak it up in my veins to free him of the bars locked inside him, caging him like a beast. Our tongues collide, the water causing slick friction and added warmth inside my mouth. Every other stroke I get closer to the edge. His back flexes with determination as he fucks me, stretches me, and ruins me for anyone else.

There's only room for one explosion in my heart, and that boom belongs to Jenkins.

"I love you," he says, burying to the hilt. There is no more room. Every scandalous inch of him is inside me. "I love you. I love you. I love you," he chants three times. It's always three times.

I clutch on to him tighter, and the water washes away a tear, one of joy and relief. "I love you, Jenkins." We hold each other up, bodies clinging to every inch of one another as his eyes search for that amazing high we can only give one another. With how his hips are moving quicker, I can tell he is close.

"I deserve her. I deserve her. I deserve her," falls from Boomer's mouth as he speaks to himself.

Oh, what's going on inside that beautiful mind? "You deserve more," I say in return, answering the loud plea in his heart.

"Jenkins," I say, my voice muddled by the water before crying out and digging my teeth into his shoulder as he expertly pulls a mind-blowing orgasm from my body.

He pumps into me, groaning, telling me he loves me so many times. I wonder if he thinks he'll never get the opportunity to say it again. I want to hear it for as long as I live. He plants himself inside me, holding me with so much force I know I'll have bruises on my hips tomorrow. The water turns cold, but his cum is hot and splashes against my sensitive, trembling walls.

We stand there, a shaking mess from the climaxes and cold water. He places kisses all over my chest before leaning back and turning the knobs off. The spray comes to a halt, and we stand there, dripping and shivering, and amazingly the only thing left scalding hot is his cock inside me.

"How are you still hard?"

"You look so fucking good wet and the image of you sucking my cock," he groans and slowly pulls out of me. "Jesus, I'm taking that with me to my grave."

I slap his chest, and he stumbles back as I climb out of the shower, wrapping a towel around my body. "What was that for?"

"Talking about being in the grave. I don't like it." I point sternly then toss him a towel.

"Aw, sugar. That won't happen for a long time."

"Better not."

"Or what?" he taunts with a sly smile, wrapping one arm around my waist and the other to cup the back of my neck.

"I'll put you there myself, that's what."

"Oh, I love it when you talk all bad, sugar."

"You're impossible," I say, running the towel down my body.

"Is that so?" His hands fall to my ribs and start tickling me.

"No! Boomer!" I laugh uncontrollably and try to get away from him. I can't breathe. Tears are in my eyes, and I manage to get away and jump to the other side of the bed. I'm gasping for breath from the assault, and he stands there, hands flat on the bed, rocking from side to side on his foot like he's about to take off like a rocket and get to me. "Don't even think about it." I look around for a weapon, anything to keep him from tickling me. He leans back and holds his hands out at the ready, nine fingers wiggling. I see his backpack on the table and grab it. "I'll throw it."

"Oh, I'm so scared. I'm shaking," he mocks in a teasing tone, taking a step to his right to come around the bed. Instead of running like I expect him to, he jumps and lands at the perfect angle to tickle me. I'm not even laughing at this point because I can't breathe. I hate being ticklish. I hit him with his bag over and over again to get him off me, and the bag breaks, emptying its contents onto him.

My laughter dies down when I see a black vest, shiny like leather, reminding me of the men who took me. "What is that?" I ask, reaching for it. He tries to snatch it away, but I'm quicker. It is leather. It smells like it, rich and musky. I hold it up, and what I see makes my heart stop, and my blood turns to mud. I can barely hold myself up.

On the back is the same logo as the other vests. The skull,

the crown, the Ruthless Kings name across the top and bottom. Only it says Vegas Chapter on it instead of Atlantic City.

"Let me explain," he pleads with me, holding his hands up. His brows frown, and his eyes are sincere, but I can't stop seeing the men who took me wearing this same damn piece of leather.

I run my finger over the patch that says his name. "Boomer," in white block letters against a black patch. "You're one of them? You're one of those... monsters! You're one of them!" I scream, tossing the vest at him because it's a fucking vest, no matter how much they want to pretty it up and make it sound more badass by calling it a cut. "Do you even care? Are you going over there to have your fill of those girls? I trusted you! I trusted you!" I sob as the betrayal takes over me.

"Let me explain," he repeats and crawls across the bed to get closer to me.

"Stay away from me!" I yell, seeing the hurt across his face as if I slapped him. "You...You touched me. You told me ...you said you loved me. You said..." I bury my face in my hands. "You're a liar!" My voice breaks as a mournful wail is released.

"No, sugar, no. I do love you. It's why I didn't tell you. I wanted to protect—"

"Don't you dare!" I shove him, and he falls onto the bed. "Don't you dare say you were protecting me! Lying is no protection. It's pain you inflict on another person. You hurt me. You *are* hurting me." Maybe this is what they do; they like to hurt people any way they can, some physically, some psychologically.

The whites of his eyes turn red, and they fill with water. "I never wanted to hurt you. I love—"

"Don't you dare finish that statement." Because I want to believe it, I do, but all I see and feel are chains and rough concrete. "You and your friends ... they're your club, aren't they?"

"Yes," he says.

I run over to the dresser and get dressed, needing to get out of here before I end up in another hole with dangerous men.

"Where are you going?" Boomer stands, naked, his cock swaying as he walks to me. Why does he have to be so beautiful? He stops and clutches his head, shaking it as if there's something inside for him to get out. "Don't go, stop!" He slams his hand against the door, keeping me prisoner. I went from one jail cell to the other. "I love you, Scarlett. We aren't like them."

I want to believe him. The broken, traumatized part of me doesn't; it's telling me to run, to protect myself, while my heart is saying stay.

"Let me go," I say through clenched teeth. I need to get the others and get out of here.

"I can't do that, sugar. You can hate me; I'll live with it if it means you're safe."

The name causes my chest to hitch. "I'm not safe here."

"You're safe! You're safer with me than with anyone. I'm your safety! Please." He tries to cup my face and kiss me, but I push him away, shoving him with all my might. He stumbles and falls back, and I take the opportunity to run for it, my heart shattering into pieces. The parts that were stitched together by him will never heal again. I open the door, slam it, and break the doorknob so he's locked inside.

"Scarlett!" He bangs on the door and jiggles the handle. "Scarlett, don't do this!"

I don't have much time before he breaks down that door.

Just like he broke the wall of trust I built for him.

Ruthless Kings can never be trusted. The only thing they know how to do is ruin.

CHAPTER TWENTY-TWO

Boomer

I T'S MORNING WHEN I FINALLY WAKE UP ON THE PORCH, HEAD bleeding and my body sore from breaking through the door in the blinding rage I felt last night. I was supposed to run after her, but I ended up only hurting myself.

Now, she's gone.

She's gone.

I get up and stumble inside the room to put shorts on since I'm still naked and grab the lamp off the nightstand and throw it. "Fuck!" My sobs break free, my clarity, my healing, my calm all shattering.

The intrusive thoughts slam into me and send me to my knees. I clutch my head and try to shake them free, but they stick to me like a parasite, draining me of life.

Worthless. You're worthless. That's why she left you.

"No," I whisper and get to my feet, taking a vase off the

dresser and throwing it. "No! I'm fucking worthy. I'm worthy." I bang my chest, still sore from the resuscitation Tongue gave me.

You're a liar. You're insane. She deserves better. You should have died in that ocean. Death would be better.

Kill yourself.

Kill yourself.

Kill yourself.

"No! I'll never do that. I'll never do that. I didn't mean to do it the last time. I didn't mean it!" I pull at the hairs on my head as I unravel, the delicate strings connecting to my heart breaking. "Oh god!" I clutch my chest when pain unlike I've ever felt before puts an indescribable amount of pressure on my heart.

"Boomer!" Reaper yells, running into the room. He sees me for the pathetic, worthless, insane person I am. "Doc! Doc, you have to get in here!" Reaper falls to his knees in front of me, and I just want it to end the crazy in my head. I can't take much more. I'm so tired, and now Scarlett isn't here, my anchor. I'm a weak man, and I fucking know that.

A hard backhand across my face calms me down.

"Look at me, kid," Reaper says, tugging me up to my feet. "Look me in the fucking eyes like I taught you."

I bring my eyes up to him, the only father figure I truly remember. "She's gone, Reap. She found my cut. She's fucking gone, and I can't fucking think. It ... it's too much." I point to my temples. "I need her to breathe."

"We'll get her back, but you need to be strong for her now. Time to conquer, kid. It's time to tell yourself the opposite of whatever is in that head of yours."

Doc runs through the door, shirt off, hair a mess, and sleep in his eyes. "I'm here. I'm here; what is it."

"Good can come from this. Use it," Reaper says.

"Everything okay?" Doc asks. "You're bleeding."

Reaper and I stare at each other, and the need to set something on fire or to blow something or someone up hits me full force. With every horrid thought, I do what Reaper says and tell myself the opposite.

"There he is," Reaper says, slapping my arm. "That's who we need tonight."

"I have to go find Scarlett, Reap. I don't know where she is."

A few of the other guys trickle in, and I'm surprised when I see Melissa standing next to Poodle. Joanna and Abigale stand next to each other with Wolf on the right side of them. The girls are here, which means they didn't want to go with Scarlett.

"What is it?" Melissa asks. "Where's Scarlett?"

"She left," I say on a pissed off snarl.

Everyone is up in a roar, talking over each other and yelling. "Stop! Just stop," I shout and grab the shirt of mine Scarlett wore last night. It smells just like her. Flowery and light. "Bitching about it won't get us anywhere," I tell them, throwing on my cut then armoring myself with my weapons of choice. "I'm done waiting around for the right time. We go there. We fuck them up. We obliterate them." I push through Reaper, Tool, Bullseye and the rest of the crew and make my way toward my bike. That's when I notice one of the men from the other chapter talking to Homer. "Tell the girls to stay back, Wolf too." I haul down the hall when the guy slams Homer against the wall, and the old man crumbles to the ground. How the hell can someone do that? The man grins down at Homer. The heavy thud of my boots against the ground must bring his attention to me charging forward because his eye meet mine in challenge.

I lift my fist and smashing him in the face. "You son of a bitch!"

He laughs as I hit him, blood coating his teeth. "Go ahead. Hit me." He leans up and gives me a knowing grin. "Getting rid of me won't bring Scarlett back. Little bitch is stupid wandering on the road on her own. I saw that tight ass and brought her where she belonged."

I smash his head against the pavement, hearing the skull crack. It isn't enough to shut him up. I knew they would get her if she left me. I knew it.

"You think Venom believed your shit? You think you're so high up. Fuck you."

"Fuck me?" I smash his head in again and hold out my hand. Tongue gives me a knife, his knife, and I'm so glad I didn't have to ask for a weapon. My guys just know. I cut the corner of his mouth into a frown, and he shrieks in agony. He resembles a ventriloquist doll. It suits him, doing whatever Venom tells him to. I spit in his face. "Fuck you, you dirty son of a bitch. You come here to send a message? They only send you?"

He lulls his head from left to right, the twitch of his eyes telling me he probably has brain damage. "It's because they don't give a flying fuck about you. They knew we would kill you, and you know what? I'm going to send a message in return." I pull out a grenade, and a flashback of my first kill filters through my mind. "What do you think happens when someone gets blown up?" I inch my face toward his, licking my lips when I remember the spray of all the blood it creates. "I bet there's a moment of horrible anticipation, like any second you're going to die, but which second? I love waiting to find out." Giving in to my urges, those thoughts turn silent. I know my problem now.

I just need to give into the side of me that no one would love, and I'll be who I need to be, who my guys need me to be; who she needs me to be.

If I have to sacrifice my sanity to keep Scarlett safe, then I'll gladly lose my mind, numbing my heart to anything but fucking pain and blood.

"Homer is okay, just knocked out. Tough old bastard," Doc says from behind me.

I have a better idea. "Tongue?" I tuck my grenade back in my pocket and wipe the blood from his knife on my shorts. "Want to do the honors? We're going to send him back since Venom wanted to send a message. He'll see just how unforgiving we really are, and then later…" I bend down and pick the man up by his cut and rip his patches off. "…I'm going to shove that grenade in your mouth. You can count the seconds until your ability to think is gone. Boom. Over. I look forward to our date." I look at his patch and snort. "Skidmark."

Tongue takes the blade from my hand, spinning it around in his fingers. He pretends to bite Skidmark like a dog, clamping his jaws together to crack his teeth. He cackles with glee and lightning bolts across the sky, matching Tongue's fury. "Oh, it's been so long," his slow Southern voice appreciates in excitement. "You know why the call me Tongue?" The crazy bastard sits on the man's chest to keep him still, and he reaches into his mouth to pull that red appendage out. "I fucking love making assholes like you go mute."

"Fuck, I can't watch this," Poodle cringes and turns his back.

I'm not going to take my eyes off him. I'm going to relish in the one thing I've denied myself for far too long. Skidmark cries as Tongue jabs the knife right through the middle, then he yanks it forward, splitting the man's tongue in half. Blood is everywhere, coating Tongue's hands and jeans. His head is back, roaring like a god who just received his first sacrifice. Tongue brings the blade up to his nose, inhaling the unmistakable iron scent, and moans.

The man cries, trying to cover his mouth with his hands, but Tongue isn't having that. He grabs the split, useless muscle in that man's mouth and cuts it off, leaving him choking on his own blood as it fills his throat.

"That's it, spit it all out. Go ahead," Tongue cheers as the guy coughs up a fountain of blood. "Just like that." The tongue gets tossed in the air and lands with a slap on the concrete, quickly staining it red.

"Come on. Let's go shut down this chapter once and for all," I say, suddenly feeling like a leader, like I mean something more than just being in the club. I want to have a high position. I want to be the one people call on if they need something in hot ashes.

"Bullseye, take him back. Be unseen. Dump him," Reaper orders, and Bullseye nods, picking up the useless body and throwing it over his shoulder as he gets into Homer's Bronco.

"What are we going to do with the girls?" Wolf says. "They can't be here alone."

"They stay here with you." I watch as Bullseye pulls out of the parking lot and drives away.

"What? No, I want to be there."

"They trust you," I say, leaning forward. "That's a big deal. They need you here."

"Are we sure we want to do this without the rest of the guys?" Tool asks. "We're letting this twenty-year-old, no offense, barely stable boy run the fucking show? Doesn't it seem a little off to you?"

"Who's stable here, Tool? Tongue just cut out a man's, well, tongue, and you carry around a screwdriver because it does *everything*. Bullseye kills people with darts. Knives is kind of like Tongue; only he likes to cut people up and not cut things out. Slingshot carries a slingshot—" Poodle sticks up for me again, and Reaper stops his rambling.

"We get it, Poodle. We get it."

"Well, I'm just saying maybe Tool needs to come off his high horse. No one is perfect."

Tool pushes off the wall and goes to charge at Poodle, but Reaper holds him back. "Don't be mad at him because he's right. Put that anger elsewhere. We need to plan. Going in there and fucking things up doesn't ever work. Someone will always get killed."

"I'm tired of waiting. You heard that guy! Venom has Scarlett. What would you do if—"

"Kid, I've lived this. Don't you forget?" Reaper reminds me.

"I know, I'm sorry, okay? I need her back." I need her safe.

"We will get her. We always win."

"Good evil versus bad evil?" I ask, wondering if there is such a thing.

"Whatever it is, it's still good, ain't it?" Reaper asks. "Here's what I think. We go in and empty out that damn shed. Those poor bastards don't have long. Doc, you're going to have to get a big van to fit all the wounded. The guys hanging in the shed, the girls, they're first before any of us, so if any of you get wounded, suck it the fuck up. I don't care if Boomer blows your arm off; you aren't priority."

"Got it, Prez," Doc says, patching up Homer's head. The old man keeps swatting at Doc's hand, but doc ignores him.

"Boomer, how much artillery do you have?" Reaper asks, and all eyes turn on me.

"Enough to soothe my itch," I reply, patting all the pockets I made for my cut to feel the weight of the short dynamite sticks I have. They're big enough to fit right in someone's mouth. I can't wait to use them.

"And they call me crazy," Tongue says, sitting on the ground as he sharpens his knife and cleans it off to a perfect polished shine.

"Says the guy bathed in blood from cutting out someone's tongue," Badge grumbles.

"Just doing what's expected of me." Tongue lifts a shoulder, not caring about what anyone has to think about him.

I'm finally at that point too.

I'm done letting my vice control me.

I'm going to control it, and the violent thoughts? Fuck 'em because they're about to be violent tendencies that will help me battle a war.

A war I plan on conquering.

CHAPTER TWENTY-THREE

Scarlett

I WISH I COULD TURN THE CLOCK BACK A DAY AND LISTEN TO THE part of soul that told me to stay with Boomer. I knew I made a mistake the second I stepped foot on that highway and started walking toward the city where all the casinos are. I saw the truth in his eyes, the hurt, the pain.

He lied to protect me, and I turned around and did something worse.

I hurt him on purpose.

Now, I'm back where it all started, only I'm not in the basement. I'm in Venom's room, chained to the bed, spread eagle. Luckily, I'm not naked, but I know it's only a matter of time before he has his way.

Stupid. I'm so stupid. I deserve what I get for leaving Boomer like that. I wouldn't listen to reason, to anything, and it was dumb of me. I'm glad the girls didn't agree to come with me; no matter how much I begged them, they wouldn't move.

Smart women.

Or they would be like me right now, bound on a dirty bed with sheets that reek of sweat and sex. And I know it wasn't consensual. No woman in their right mind would willingly have sex with Venom.

My arms ache from being pulled back, and the collar around my throat is tighter this time. I'm not panicking. I'm scared, yes, but panic... that I don't feel. Maybe it's because I know my fate. I regret not telling Boomer how much I love him or how sorry I am for not believing in him.

A commotion from outside the bedroom door gets my attention. I hone in the best I can, trying to figure out what is going on. A slight knock on the window has me turning my head to the left, staring through the dust shining against the sun beaming through the glass. The collar pinches my throat and mildly cuts off my air supply.

But I've never felt more relieved. Bullseye is there; I think that's his name. He holds up his phone and puts his finger to his lips, telling me to be quiet. He must be telling someone I'm alright. Maybe Boomer? Maybe somehow, someway, he still cares even though I've betrayed him now, his trust, his faith, his love.

Maybe there's still a chance for us.

The door busts in, and Bullseye dips down so Venom doesn't see him. My eyes round, and I try to get away from him when I see him holding up a man who looks dead, dried blood around his mouth. Venom's chest is pumping, a sheen of sweat either from anger or the lack of not having air conditioning, shines against his chest, and he points at me.

"Look what your fucking men did to mine!" he roars,

dragging the body by the scalp. He puts the man right against the bed and pries his mouth open. "You see that! Do you see what those fuckers did?"

They cut out his tongue.

"And half of his fucking skull is bashed in. They've declared war. They have no idea who they're messing with. They think I can't smell deceit. Reaper has always been a good boy. I knew when he showed up he was up to no good. Good thing I had my boys follow him around. I didn't think anything of it until I saw you and that boy fucking on the beach." He throws the dead man onto the floor, the skull landing with a loud thud, and it makes me flinch. "Is that what I have to do to you, girly? I gotta fuck you? If I knew you were handing it out so easy, I wouldn't have put you in the basement with the rest." He cups my pussy, and there's nothing I can do. I'm at his mercy while I'm bound to the iron bed.

At least I'm not naked. Small favors and all.

"I bet this pussy is sweet," he howls. "And when I'm done, I'm going to have my men take their turn. They'll fill you up with so much cum, you'll probably get pregnant and won't know who the baby daddy is." He laughs, running his nicotine-stained fingers down my leg. "All while you're tied up with nowhere to go. Eventually, I'll do to you what they did to him." He points to the dead man on the ground. "But not before I have a taste of you."

"Fuck you." I spit a wad of saliva at him, and it lands on his face.

He swipes his finger through it and puts it in his mouth, somersaulting my stomach into a chaotic knot. Bile creeps up my throat when he smiles, showing his yellow rotted teeth. His hair is long, too long, down to his waist, and so thin I can see his scalp. "Just a taste to hold me over until later." He throws his head back and laughs, slamming the door behind him as he leaves.

He forgot to take the dead guy with him. I swallow, keeping my head turned so I don't have to see him face-up, mouth open, with no tongue. It's disturbing and enough to add to the nightmares I'll have for the rest of my life.

I glance at the window again, but there's no sign of Bullseye. I hoped he was coming to take me away, but nothing is ever that simple. If life was so easy, this situation wouldn't exist, not for me or anyone.

A light tap on the window gets my attention again, and Bullseye's head pop up. I see the smear of blood on his cheek. He smiles and holds up something small and green. He yanks the clip off and throws it to the left of him. He rubs his hands together and then lifts three up.

Then two.

Holy shit, he's counting down. I brace myself.

One.

An explosion rocks the house, and Bullseye sends me a wink before dunking below the window again. It's like pop goes the freaking weasel with that guy. Will he stop playing around and get me out of here?

He pops up and punches through the glass, a shirt wrapped around his hand, and surprisingly, it makes less noise. He reaches in and opens it from the inside and climbs in, careful to keep himself quiet.

"Good to see you're still in once piece," he says, hurrying over to my side and inserts a dart into the lock.

"That's not going to wo—" The lock sliding free catches me by surprise. He gets to work on the lock on my wrist and neck. Soon, I'm free, and Bullseye hands me a dart. "Listen up because I don't have much time before shit hits the fan. We're going to climb out the window, and you're—"

But he doesn't have time to finish. Venom kicks the door in and lifts a gun, shooting Bullseye right in the chest. I feel the warm spray of blood against my face and kneel to check on him when Venom grabs me by the hair, dragging me out of the room on my knees.

"Let me go!" I scream, fighting to break free of his hold.

"I'll make sure he won't get you," he seethes, opening up the basement door that swallowed me whole to begin with. He throws me down the steps, and my arm bends at a funny angle as I hit the middle step. I cry out, continuing to roll down the stairs, my body hitting each sharp edge with more force than the last. "You'll die here. I'll make sure of that." The light that casted down the steps is gone when he slams the door shut.

"Are you okay?" a soft voice asks from my right. "Miss?"

I groan, pushing myself up on my good arm. My bone is sticking out. I'm in so much pain that I almost can't feel it. The white spear is covered in blood, and my arm is throbbing. My red life force is pooling on the ground quickly. I need a temporary fix, and the only way is to pop the bone back in. "I'm going to get you all out of here," I say through broken gasps. "First, does anyone have a belt?"

"I do," a girl in the back says.

I fall over myself trying to get to her, nearly running into a slanted beam that's about to give. If it does, the entire house will collapse on us. I fall to my knees, feeling a bit woozy from either the blood loss or the fact I see the bone sticking out of my arm.

"What's it for?" she asks.

"For me to bite down on because this is going to hurt." I might end up doing myself more harm than good, but I can't get these girls out of here with my bone out. Fuck, what about Bullseye? I need to get to him too. This is all fucked up. How is this so fucked up!

I fumble with her belt, and it takes some doing since I can only use one hand. It's a skinny belt, made to be fashionable, but it's better than nothing. "Okay. Okay. Alright," I tell myself. "We're doing this. You, can I borrow that cardigan?"

"Yes, go ahead. I don't freaking need it. Just get us out of here!"

I yank the cardigan off her and shove the belt in my mouth. I shake my head; I can't do this. I can't. I cry when the wound burns from the agony. I'm horrible with pain, but these girls need me. I have to push through it.

"On the count of three," the girl says, who's now wearing a camisole, showing the bruises along her arms.

I nod to her, glad that she's taking control, or we would be here all night.

"One."

I take a breath.

"Two."

I send a silent prayer to somebody, anyone who will listen.

"Three!"

I shove the bone back in my skin, my muscles being pinched and pushed. The swollen tissue and broken veins sting and burn with so much pain. I fall onto my ass and scream around the belt, biting through the cheap plastic, and everything around me tilts and spins.

"Oh god, that sounded sick. Jesus, are you okay?"

I don't answer her. I try to regulate my breathing by

making my lungs expand. I fight the urge to pass out and sit up. With sloppy movements as if I were drunk, I wrap the cardigan around my arm, then create a makeshift sling. "I need a minute," I say, falling against the rickety beam. It groans, and I move off it, falling to my knees. The dart moves in my pocket, poking me in the leg, and that's when I remember Bullseye giving it to me before he got shot. He counted on me. He gave it to me for a reason, and I bet it was so I could get these girls out.

I reach in and take the metal dart out and unlock the collar around the girl who let me have her cardigan. "What's your name?"

"Mary," she chokes when the collar falls free. "Thank you."

"Help is coming," I say. "Just give them time." Another explosion rings out, and dirt falls down on us like rain.

Time we might not have.

I hurry with all of their locks, and by the end of it, I'm sweating, swallowing down mouthfuls of vomit from the pain and exertion I'm putting myself through. We sit near the steps in the corner and wait, hoping that the next explosion doesn't bury us alive.

CHAPTER TWENTY-FOUR

Boomer

"**C**OMING IN FUCKING HOT!" I YELL, GRABBING ANOTHER piece of shit man that dares call himself a Ruthless and shove a stick of dynamite down his throat. He doesn't even have time to think and I love the moment they realize that.

All wide-eyed and afraid.

Reaper has his gun, shooting the enemy down one by one. Bodies lay everywhere, resembling a graveyard.

I take a grenade and throw it on the front porch at the time two men run out right as the bomb goes off. "Eight down," I tell myself, but who is counting?

I see Tongue in the distance, climbing out of the window with a massive body slung over his shoulder. Fuck, that's Bullseye.

"Bullseye is down! Shot in the chest!"

Reaper stops shooting when he hears that, earning him his own bullet right in the shoulder. He cries out, lifting the weapon with the same arm he is shot in. God, I hope to be as badass as him one day. He fires at the man, landing two bullets in his head.

Someone's wraps their arms around me, trying to choke the life out of me. I rear my arm up and slam it back, using my elbow to break a rib. I grab another grenade and shove it in the front of the guys pants, letting a mad laugh escape me when I hear the loud *bang* blowing off his dick.

Sucks to be him.

Tool and Knives open the doors that allow people into the basement. One by one, Tool helps the girls, but I don't see Scarlett. I look around, searching the area for any sign of her, but she isn't there. Most of the enemy is down, dead, and only a few remain. Those who do are on their knees pleading for their life.

"Please," the bastard begs. "Please. I never agreed with what he did."

I pull out a knife, not wanting to hear his excuses and shove it right in his head. I yank it out and a sickening crush sounds from his skull and brain turning to mush. I kick him down with my father's boot and seeing that, feeling his cut on me, a new sense of power overcomes me. It feels stronger than usual, like him, like my dad.

I don't believe in that shit, but right now, I'm willing to believe in anything. I charge toward the front of the broken front door, not bothering to look as I slice another throat. I'm covered in sweat, blood, and dirt.

And I'll continue on my fucking wrath until I have what I came here for.

My clarity.

Right as I go to open the door, a man tackles me from the side, and it allows me to catch a glimpse of Tool and Badge opening the shed. I don't have time to look for more, to see if they got those guys out because this guy manages to get his hands wrapped around my throat, a lucky move on his part. He sticks his tongue out, a crazy gleam in his eyes as he watches my face turn red.

The knife is knocked out of my hand and I can't get to my grenades. I reach up and dig my fingers into his eyes, pushing them so far into their socket, they start to bleed. The man jumps off me and cries, "I'm blind. I'm blind!"

"It's the least of your worries." I grab my knife and sling it, landing right in the man's throat. I walk over and pull it out, allowing the blood to bathe my boots as it flows out of him, just like a dam breaking. "How's it feels? The pressure in your throat?" I watch as he realizes he is about to die and right as the last second ticks by, his pupils round and dilate.

Dead.

It's starting to get quiet, too quiet because Venom has yet to be seen. The porch is fucked, so I have to jump up to grab the floor where the front door used to be and pull myself up. Grunting, my throat still burning from the man's hands, I walk inside.

My boots leave a red trail in their wake and when I get to the main room, Venom is there, sitting at a poker table, a gun to Scarlett's temple and a deck of cards in a neat stack. Her hands are bound, and that damn collar is on her again. I fucking swear, I'm not going to kill this guy. I'm going to put the collar around his neck chain him naked to two trucks and tell who is ever driving to gas it so I can see him get ripped to fucking shreds from the base of his neck.

"Things are getting out of hand, don't you think?" Venom exhales a cloud of smoke, thick with a green tint and by the skunk smell of it, I'd say it's weed.

I pull a chair out and notice how bad Scarlett is shaking. Tears are running down her face and she looks at me with so much love, fear, and apology, begging me to get her out of here. And I will, but no fast moves, not when Venom has a gun to her head.

"You know, we can settle this like men," he says. "I'm all about playing for keeps, boy."

There's that fucking name again.

"Either way, you aren't walking out of here alive, Venom. I'm going to take my Old Lady there and blow you to fucking bits." Well, I'm torn on what I really want to do to him. The sicker side of me wants more for him than a quick death, but for Scarlett's sake, he deserves to never walk out of this house.

"Oh, that's not how a gentlemen's wager works. Now, we play, you win, you get your girl, and I walk free, never to bother you again."

"If I lose?"

"This sweet little piece of ass is mine."

Over my dead body. "Fine," I tell him, and Scarlett pinches her brows, shaking her head so hard that the tears fly and wet the felt on the table. He reaches his hand over for a shake and I meet it, knowing damn good and well, to never trust anyone that can lie.

"You deal," he says, placing the joint between his lips.

I deal out the community cards in a line straight in the middle and deal out two cards to each of us. There is no betting or throwing money down because Scarlett is the prize. When I peek at the cards in my hand, I hide my grin. I have the best fucking poker face there is. And I know that the only one leaving here a winner, is me.

Venom chuckles. "Ah, kid, sucks to be you. I can't wait to sink into this tight cunt." He lays out his two cards and he is right, it isn't bad, but mine is better. Nothing can beat mine. He has two Aces.

"Yeah," I drawl out, "but the only man sinking into her tight cunt, will be me." I lay down my hand and show that I have a royal flush. "Who is the king now, Venom?"

His jaw tics and in a quick move he throws Scarlett at me, the points the gun to my head. I duck down and barely miss the bullet and rip the clip of the grenade off with my teeth. Scarlett stares at the device, knowing that we are going to have to haul ass. I stand up and throw it at his feet, watching the confusion, then realization, then acceptance roll over his features.

I grab Scarlett and do our best to run out, but the grenade goes off, sending us flying in the air. We land in the dirt outside and she's clutching her arm, sobbing.

"You okay?" I pick her up, and she throws her arms around me.

"I'm so sorry, Boomer. I'm so sorry. I love you. I love you so much. I wasn't think—"

I silence her with a passionate kiss, diving my tongue between her lips. That crazy fucking haze in my head lifts, but part of me is more settled than ever. I've come to terms with who I am and what I need.

And what I need is this MC life.

"Go with Tool. I'm going to make sure he's dead," I tell her. "I love you, Scarlett. Don't ever fucking do that to me again."

"Never," she says quickly.

Tool guides her away to the van that's nearly full to capacity with people who need medical attention. I turn back to the house and lift myself up like before. The floor is gone, smoke lingers, and when I get to where Venom was, all that's left are his boots and the smoking aces he thought he had me with.

"Ready to burn this bitch to the ground?" Reaper says, carrying in a few gallons of gasoline. We're hoping Wolf and the guys who were taken down from the shed know more about this operation. Hopefully, it was only an issue at this chapter, and our job is done.

"Who you talking to, Reap? I was born ready to burn shit."

Reaper kicks a jug, and it slides over to me. I unscrew the top and start to pour, and the strong fumes make my cock twitch. I bend over and grab the half-fried aces that still have a burning ember to them. I dust them against my pants and keep them as trophies. It's my biggest accomplishment yet.

"Tongue is piling the bodies and then will burn those. Soon, this place will be nothing but a memory," Reaper says.

We pour until the jugs are empty, then jump down from the doorstep onto the ground. "Hold on," I say, running over to Scarlett as she leans against the van while Doc is checking her arm.

"Fucking badass that you popped your bone back in—" I come in on.

"What!" I bark, and Scarlett gives me a half smile.

"I'll explain later," she hisses as Doc starts to stitch her up.

"Put that on hold, Doc." I hold up a matchbook. "Want to do the honors of lighting this place up?"

Scarlett pushes off the van, and Doc stumbles over his words when thread and needle hang from her arm. She takes the matchbook and opens it, pulls the wooden stick with a red head out, and stares at it.

BOOMER

Scarlett lowers the match to her jeans, the quick scratch sounds, and a swaying flame takes the place of the red top. Watching with desire, she flicks it inside the door, and the whoosh of a quick burning blaze spreads, flickering blue, just like Scarlett's eyes.

She's the match, the fuse, the gasoline, the kerosene, the bombs, the dynamite, the flame, the heat, and the burn.

Scarlett is by far the biggest boom I will ever experience.

My true clarity.

EPILOGUE

Boomer

A week later

WE HOLD CHURCH IN HOMER'S OFFICE. DOC IS STILL FUSSING about his bandage, and Homer still slaps his hand away.

"I ain't no pussy," Homer states, chest out and proud. "Get your hands off me."

A few men hide their chuckles behind their hands, camouflaging them with a cough. Kansas, One-eye, and Arrow are in wheelchairs, looking like fucking death with how pale they are. They're skinny from not being fed, and dehydrated. They have scars on their wrists and ankles from being tied up like a starfish in the shed. When we got to them, they were barely alive, but for some fucking reason, they didn't want to miss church.

They allowed me to burn their cuts too.

BOOMER

"This Atlantic City chapter has officially been dissolved. It no longer exists," Reaper says, knocking the stapler on the desk as a makeshift gavel. Everyone hollers and claps, and the girls hug each other and cry, smiling with happy tears. Scarlett mouths, "I love you," to me, and fuck, if I don't feel like a new man.

Homer rolls his eyes. "This is church? Hootenanny! Back where I come from that mean praising the Lord."

"You believe in God, Homer?" Poodle asks, surprised just like the rest of us.

"I said where I come from. I didn't say I went to fucking church. Open your damn ears," Homer says.

"Grumpy," Poodle pouts.

"What's next?" Kansas' voice makes everyone quiet down. It's weak, barely a whisper. "Where do we go?"

"Well, I wanted to talk to you about that, Boomer," Reaper says, grabbing a few new cuts from the box. "I don't think you're meant to come back with us, kid, no matter how much I want you to. I've watched you grow into a man while being here. Sure, you broke a few times, but we all do, and now you're who you need to be. You left to find yourself, and you did just that. You found yourself a new club, one that you can call your own. One that you can lead. You are meant for more than what I can give you."

He tosses the new cut to me and the patch says, "President" and another says "Boomer."

"But... how am I going to build a club? What about you all? What about Sarah?"

"I've talk to everyone, kid, even Kansas, Arrow, and One-Eye. They all voted on it. You're the Prez."

"What? But I don't think it's a good idea to bring Ruthless

here again, Reaper. The city, the people who owe that club, they'll never believe we're the good guys."

"It's why I left the back blank. It's up to you. We can be allies. You're meant to be here, kid. You've done good. Look at all you accomplished. These women, those men, they're alive and well because of you."

I look at all of them, nodding to give me reassurance. I stop at Scarlett when I see she has a cut in her hand. I tilt my head to the side in confusion and she lifts it up, showing me the "Property of" patch on it with my name under it.

Fucking hell, is this happening? It's really fucking happening.

"Your dad would be proud of you, kid. Do you want this?" Reaper asks.

"I... I ... don't have a clubhouse," I say with a chuckle.

"The fuck you mean?" Homer gripes. "I have this motel. You can turn it into whatever as long as you let me retire and live here."

"Seriously?" I ask, openmouthed.

"Yeah, I like you lot. Except you." He points to Tongue. "You creep me the fuck out."

Tongue lifts his lips in a half smirk but doesn't say a word.

"What do you say?" Homer repeats.

"I say 'fuck yeah!'" I shout, and everyone cheers along with me.

"Tonight we celebrate," Reaper yells. Scarlett saunters over to me, shrugging on her cut.

Fuck, she looks so damn sexy in that.

"You sure you want this?" I ask her.

"I want you. All of you." She grabs the side of my head, telling me she accepts me for who I am. I told her last night of my intrusive thoughts and how hard it gets to fight them. She held my hand and told me she'd fight them with me, and just knowing she's there and loves me through it only makes me love her more.

"I can't wait to fuck you in this cut. And only this cut," I growl into her ear.

"Oh, you want to go make good of that threat, Jenkins?" she purrs my name into my ear and scratches her nails down me like a cat in fucking heat.

I drag her out of the office and take her to the nearest flat surface to show her just how much I make good on my promises.

I may not be a Ruthless King anymore, but it's in my blood.

Forever.

Love. Family. Loyalty.

And *Boom*.

ACKNOWLEDGMENTS

Jenifer Briggs, your reviews and comments everywhere are always so full of emotion; you can feel it jumping off the screen. I'm honored that my Ruthless Kings do that for you.

I want to thank all the blogs and reviewers for reviewing and sharing Boomer. I know how busy reviewers' schedules can be.

Give Me Books—thanks for getting my books out there and in front of so many people. Kylie, Jo, and Alicia, you all truly go above and beyond.

Silla, you remind me to breathe. You always say "You're gonna be fine; you got this." And when I'm spreading myself too thin you say, "Breathe, I got this," and those words right there are worth more than gold! Thanks for being so great.

Kari, your designs always leave me speechless! Your vision for my covers and graphics is always perfect.

Wander, thanks for sharing your talent with the world. I still can't believe I have your images on my covers.

Andrey, your kindness makes this world a better place. I cringe just thinking of trying to tackle images without you. Thanks for always being there.

Happy Birthday, Mom!

J.H.O 5 LITTLE WORDS

Lynn—You're definitely my better half; without you, I'd be lost.

A.S.—You are the instigator to my bad decisions. You have been my soundboard, my voice of reason, and yes, my instigator. Thanks for always being there.

Harloe, Thanks for being you.

Austin, I'm so blessed to have you both in my life.

Jordan—For always getting me and understanding I'm not being antisocial; it's just one of my quirks. Thanks for letting me camp out in my room.

John Russell, cheers to shots of Patron and new beginnings!

ALSO BY K.L. SAVAGE

PREQUEL - REAPER'S RISE
BOOK ONE - REAPER
BOOK TWO - BOOMER
BOOK THREE - TOOL
BOOK FOUR - POODLE
BOOK FIVE - SKIRT
BOOK SIX - PIRATE
BOOK SEVEN - DOC
BOOK EIGHT - TONGUE

OTHER BOOKS IN THE RUTHLESS KINGS SERIES
A RUTHLESS HALLOWEEN

RUTHLESS KINGS MC IS NOW ON AUDIBLE.

CLICK HERE TO JOIN RUTHLESS READERS AND GET
THE LATEST UPDATES BEFORE ANYONE ELSE. OR
VISIT AUTHORKLSAVAGE.COM OR STALK THEM AT
THE SITES BELOW.

FACEBOOK | INSTAGRAM | RUTHLESS READERS
AMAZON | TWITTER | BOOKBUB | GOODREADS |
PINTEREST | WEBSITE

FOR UPDATES FROM K.L. SAVAGE TEXT:

KL SAVAGE

RUTHLESS ROMANCE THAT WILL *RIP* YOUR HEART OUT.

725-225-0825

Printed in Great Britain
by Amazon

72445542R00127